# Saved By An A-Town Millionaire

## Tasha Mack

**Saved By An A-Town Millionaire**

**Mailing List**

**To stay up to date on new releases, plus get information on contests, sneak peeks, and more,**

*Go To The Website Below...*

**www.colehartsignature.com**

# Prologue
## Chicago Parker

"Girl, I'm so fucking nervous. This nigga got me fucked up. I'm telling you right now, if they play with me, I'll burn this bitch down. This entire campus gon' be ashes under my feet. Let me call you back, though. I'm about to walk into the office now."

"Can I help you?" the receptionist asked without looking up.

"I'm here to see Mr. Walker."

"You can go wait in his office. He should be back in a few minutes," she instructed.

This hoe needed another job. I couldn't stand rude mothafuckas. The minute I walked into his office, a bad feeling came over me. Five minutes came and went. My stomach was in knots.

Slumped over in the tufted leather chair in front of Mr. Walker's cherry oak desk, I anxiously rubbed the beads of sweat off my forehead, using the back of my hand. The longer I waited, the more I thought of the worst possible outcome. I was aware of my actions. I'd done the unthinkable. My academic future was on the line, but I had no regrets. If I had to choose,

1

I'd do it all over again. Nobody was going to make me feel any different.

If you asked me, Mr. Walker's office was enormous and exquisite, which was over the top for a college administrator. Having attended Tilman State for almost three years, I had never been in his office. There was no reason to. Averaging a 3.8 GPA, I had been on the Dean's list several times during my tenure there. Since achieving that accomplishment, I was the girl students paid to write their papers for them. In my eyes, my education was everything, and it came before all else. I sometimes sacrificed my mental health for it.

With my eyes roaming Mr. Walker's desk, I noticed a picture frame lying face down. In one swift motion, I picked up the photo and smiled. The woman in the picture appeared to be the happiest girl in the world. She reminded me of a suburban girl. A lifestyle that I knew nothing about. I was sure that was his wife.

I could see the shiny pendulum on the grandfather clock swinging back and forth from the corner of my eye. It was almost time for my next class to start. My meeting today would determine what would happen next. I would either be attending class or moving out. Simple. The disappointment was unsettling. It was hard to walk around campus without bitches staring me down like I was in the wrong. Little did they know, my actions were justified. Hopefully, the board viewed it that way. The harsh reality was sinking in.

Suddenly, the hairs on my neck stood as I heard the door open and close behind me. I didn't bother to turn around to face Mr. Walker. His expensive cologne greeted me before he even had the chance to open his mouth. He glanced down at the photo. Deep in thought, I'd forgotten to place the picture back on his desk where I'd found it.

"Ms. Parker, I hate we must meet under these circumstances. Can I get you anything?"

His dark eyes roamed over my body. They told a story of deception. I knew he was a powerful man. That much couldn't be denied. However, Mr. Walker wasn't who everyone thought he was. Shit, I learned firsthand, but that wasn't none of my business.

*The nerve of this mothafucka to ask me if I wanted anything. Yeah, a fucking decision that ruled in my favor,* I thought. Even though I was thirsty, I didn't want a damn thing Mr. Walker had to offer. I had to mentally check myself for fear of saying something wrong before replying no. Grabbing the picture from my hand, he smirked and placed it upright on his desk like nothing happened.

"Are you sure? I have bottles of water over there in the fridge," he offered.

"I said no," I firmly responded with a bit more authority. I wouldn't take a bottle of water from him if I was burning in the pits of hell. I'd much rather suffer.

"Fine, suit yourself. I just figured you might need it. You know it's rude to touch other people's things without asking," he taunted.

Pursing my lips together, I rolled my eyes without attempting to hide my frustration. All the small talk was starting to piss me off, and I wanted nothing more than to call Mr. Walker every name in the book but a child of God.

"Hmph. It seems you would know all about that, huh?" I smirked but quickly remembered why I was there.

I humbled myself before I wrote a check my ass couldn't cash. Mr. Walker was the wrong person for me to be brazen with. However, the nigga deserved it. He didn't give a fuck about nobody but himself.

"Ms. Parker, the board has unanimously decided to expel

you for the remainder of the school year. While re-entry won't be possible here, you may want to consider other options. I've curated a list of schools you might want to apply to with a similar academic structure," he explained, handing me a piece of paper.

My eyes grew wide with surprise. Although I knew this was possible, I never expected those words to leave Mr. Walker's lips. Since a little girl, I had dreamed of attending this college. Everything I'd done up to my high school graduation had been well thought out. From the day I knew I could get out of Chicago and choose what schools I wanted to apply to, I'd been strategic about every move. Now this man was telling me it was all over.

His mouth was still moving, but I struggled to process his words. I could feel the anger slowly rising in my chest. My nostrils flared as I stood to my feet. I could no longer contain my rage. Now that I knew my fate, I had a few choice words for his ass. Chicago was about to rear her ugly head.

"Fuck you and this school. You can take those options and shove them up your ass!"

Without reading over the paper, I slammed it on his desk, grabbed my book bag, and left his office. I didn't give a fuck about recommendations. What HBCU in their right mind would consider admitting me into their school after this shit? My heart was broken. I didn't want to hear about options. Tilman was the only option for me, and that was final. There had to be a way around this shit.

"Not so fast, Ms. Parker. Let's not forget that if you apply to another school, you need a letter of recommendation. I'd hate to tell them how disrespectful and unruly you are when things don't go your way," he countered, following me.

Stopping dead in my tracks, I turned around to face him. I wasn't stupid. Something told me he had much influence on

4

the board's decisions. Walker had it out for me, and I didn't blame him. I knew more about his personal life than he wanted, which pissed him off. It made him despise me.

Now, he was fucking with me. Mr. Walker was about to witness me turn into the Chi I'd suppressed for the past few years. His calling me disrespectful and unruly was triggering. That part of me had been buried deep within. I didn't want to be the angry black girl, but that was what this would turn into.

"Are you threatening me?"

His dark eyes roamed over my body once more. Feeling uncomfortable, I quickly turned on my heels and walked away. Once I reached the nearest restroom, my face was soaked with the tears I fought to hold back. Memories of that night caused my chest to heave up and down. Without realizing it, I'd had a full-blown panic attack. Leaning over the sink for support, I glanced at myself in the mirror.

"Okay, just take a deep breath, Chi," I whispered, attempting to coach myself.

I'd never been diagnosed with anxiety, but it didn't take much to figure out what was happening to me. I rubbed my sweaty palms against my denim jeans. The constant thumping in my chest made me feel like it would cave in. Turning the faucet on, I splashed cool water on my face to help bring down my elevated body temperature. My hands shook as I pressed a paper towel against my face.

Making it back to my room in record time, I quickly pulled out my suitcases and started stuffing them with whatever would fit. I didn't care to organize shit. If I could take all my shit and burn this bitch down, I would. Effective immediately, I was instructed to vacate the premises: no warning, no time frame, nothing. Mr. Walker made sure of that with his dirty ass. I was expected to get my shit and move on with my life. Like I didn't have fucking dreams or aspirations to achieve.

I tried my best not to be hurt by the situation, but this was the future I'd carefully mapped out for myself. Now, my journey had been cut short. There was nobody I could call on. I had to figure shit out on my own.

Due to a lack of help, I paid a moving company to pick up my things since I wouldn't have enough room in my car. It took almost everything I had in my bank account, but I had to do what was necessary. Thank goodness I paid up my storage for the remainder of the year. That was one less problem I had to worry about.

The movers weren't scheduled for another few hours, giving me plenty of time to pack everything up. After loading up my car, I took in the scenery around me. This would be the last time I stepped foot in this facility. After three years, it was over. I wasn't sure how to feel about that. I reluctantly trudged back inside after standing there, reflecting for a few minutes. Once I returned to the dorm I shared with my best friend, Demi, I broke down crying. The floodgates had opened, and I could no longer hold back the tears. Devastation consumed my entire body. With saddened eyes, she walked toward me with outstretched arms and pulled me in for a hug.

"I'm so sorry, Chi. I tried talking to him. He says it was the board's decision."

I hated when she talked about him. Demi deserved so much better. I guess she figured since they had been fucking since our first year of college, it would make a difference in his decision. I appreciated her for trying. I knew now wasn't the time to pick arguments, but I didn't care. I felt some type of way.

"Don't you think you deserve better?"

"Chi, please. That's my man. Period!"

With Dion, Demi lacked the good sense God gave her. If he said jump, she would ask how high. The constant manipulation on his end was alarming. Demi thought he was charming and didn't see things as I did. She continuously made excuses for his poor behavior.

"Demi, he's fucking married!"

"He's leaving his wife."

This was the shit that drove me crazy. It wasn't my situation, but I cared about Demi. We'd been friends since our first year, and I only wanted better. Obviously, I cared more about how he treated her than she did.

"He's not leaving her, Demi. It's been three years."

Scoffing, she picked up my bags and placed them by the door. My mind tried to comprehend what was happening. How the fuck was she mad at me for being a friend and being honest? Shit, it was the truth. Dion was only stringing her along because he was never leaving his wife. Plus, she looked like a kept bitch. One who waited on her man hand and foot and did whatever he told her to. I guess she knew of his infidelity and probably didn't care. If she disregarded her husband's blatant disrespect, she could continue to live the lifestyle he provided.

I let Demi have her moment, as she did every time I brought up the conversation. The only difference was that I didn't have the energy to go back and forth with her over the obvious. I had my own shit to deal with, like where I would stay. Chicago was the last place I wanted to go, but that appeared to be my only option. I never thought I'd see myself going back to the projects. As far as I knew, those days were behind me.

"It's bad enough *your man* put me out. Now you over here rushing along the process. It's cool, though." I fumed, snatching my bag out of her hand.

She cut her eyes. "I'm just trying to help. That's what friends do, right?" She smirked.

Little did she know, I didn't need her help. It wasn't like I could depend on her anyway. Charae had conditioned me to look after myself long ago. Her hot ass was probably somewhere turning a trick for a bottle of Paul Mason. Without speaking to Demi, I grabbed what I could and exited. The way I felt, it was best I waited in the car for the moving company before I slapped the shit out of Demi.

An hour later, the movers showed up. There was no need for me to move anything. All I had to do was meet them at my storage unit. As bad as I didn't want to go, I was ready for the twelve-hour drive back to Chicago. No matter how much of a trash mother Charae had been, she taught me how to survive. Even if I had to sleep in my car, I would make shit shake.

My phone buzzed, pulling me out of my thoughts. A Chicago number I didn't recognize flashed across the screen. I ignored the call and focused on the movers to ensure they weren't manhandling my shit. My phone buzzed again. Irritated, I answered.

"Who is this?"

"Chi, it's me. Ms. Althea."

Althea had lived in the Walker Projects for as long as I could remember. Charae once told me she'd been there since she was a child living with her mother. Althea was the neighborhood grandma and was the one person everybody knew not to disrespect.

"Oh, hey, Ms. Althea. How have you been?" There was a long pause on her end. "Is everything okay?"

"Well, I'm afraid I have some bad news, baby. Your mother has been killed in an accident."

# Chapter 1
## *Chi*

*Three years later*

"So, you telling me that bitch fired you because your car stopped while on the way to work? It's not like you intentionally tried to call out. Yo' ass should've called me. I would've taken you to work, Chi. You get on my nerves with the independent shit like you can't ask anybody for help. See, you need to work in the shop with us. We need another stylist anyway," Royce rambled.

I hated when she tried to call me out. Royce was hell-bent on making my problems her own. Although I appreciated the gesture, I was a grown woman, perfectly capable of dealing with my own shit. I wore my independence like a badge of honor. Despite things not turning out how I'd envisioned, I was thankful that I was no longer sleeping in my car.

This wasn't the first nor the second time I'd called off work due to my car issues. Instead of sympathizing, my supervisor told me not to worry about coming back. I didn't care, however. The job didn't pay enough for me to be stressed out.

"Royce, we talked about this. I'm not coming to work in that funky ass shop." It was hard to tell Royce, no, but I refused to compromise.

"And we're talking about it again. Now finish telling me what happened."

Flopping down on the bed, I rolled my eyes. For every little problem I had, Royce's first solution was for me to work at the salon. When I was first expelled from Tilman, Royce convinced me to come to Atlanta. I slept in her dorm undetected since she didn't have a roommate.

"Anyway, that's exactly what she did. I ain't tripping, though. I'll find something new. Plus, I was tired of working in that call center anyway." I exhaled, purposely ignoring the shop comment.

"I wish you and Arrington could hash things out. You two haven't seen each other in a long time. You've been in Atlanta for three years now. Something has got to give."

Growing up, I spent summers in Atlanta with my father, his wife, Tracy, and her daughter, Arrington. That was until the feds picked him up on drug charges. When he got knocked, Tracy sent my ass on the first thing smoking back to Chicago. After that, I never spent another summer there. I didn't care about leaving because I couldn't stand Tracy or her daughter. When my dad was around, Tracy would act like this loving stepmom, but she was anything but that. Her whole demeanor would change as soon as my father left the house. She was awful. Whenever I tried to tell him how Tracy treated me, he always brushed it off, which caused me to develop hatred for him.

Arrington and I never got along, so my father allowed Royce to come over, so we wouldn't cut each other's throats. Royce was cool with Arrington but would check her in a heartbeat when it came to me. Whenever we were into it, Royce was always the peacemaker. In a way, I hated that shit because we would never be more than cordial. It made me cringe, referring to that bitch as my stepsister. She was a fucking demon seed who belonged in the fiery pits of hell.

While staying with Royce, she urged me to start cosmetology school since I already knew how to do hair. Instead of finishing her year at Spelman, she dropped out and decided to join me. We took our school money and rented our first apartment together; the rest was history. I still lived in that same apartment, but Royce had moved out. She currently had a condo with her girlfriend, Alex, whom she'd been dating for the past two years.

"Bitch, you sound crazy. I wouldn't spit on that bitch if she was on fire, let alone work beside her in the shop."

"Chi, just work in the shop until you find something else. What if you start getting behind on your bills? I know you don't want to be around Arrington, but it's better than returning to the strip club," Royce suggested.

Becoming a licensed cosmetologist was never in my plan. It was something to do to make money. Even though I could slay some hair, it wasn't my passion. The strip club was a whole different story. When I moved back to Atlanta, I needed to make some fast money to help keep myself afloat, so I became exactly who I told my mother I wouldn't become. A stripper. Just like her. The only difference was that I didn't depend on drugs or alcohol to get me through.

The naked hustle saw me through some of the most challenging times. I shook my ass and didn't have to sleep with niggas to make extra money. Instead, I installed wigs in the dressing room before each set. I wasn't a top earner because I was a little thicker than the other girls. However, my face card never declined. I was beautiful, and I knew it. A skinny bitch couldn't tell me shit. A little fupa never hurt anybody. I was that girl. Period.

"Who said I was going back there? Now you are taking shit too far." I laughed.

The strip club was out of the question. I only worked there for five months before Royce approached me with the cosmetology school idea. At the time, it was the only thing that made sense. I wanted to get out of the club before it swallowed me whole. I saw it firsthand with Charae and feared I would become her if I stayed.

"I'm serious. I'll even let you do my client's installs, and I can do the cuts."

Royce specialized in cutting and knew how to shape and transform hair on a different level. Why she was still working at Bella Luxe Salon was still a mystery to me. She had enough clientele and potential for her own shop or salon suite.

"Girl, what is with you and this shop? My answer is final." I laughed. "Anyway, let me get off this phone and look for a job."

"All right, but think about what I said. You know you want t—"

"Bye, Royce." I sighed, cutting her off.

Pulling out my laptop, I updated my resume and posted it to my profile. Hopefully, it wouldn't take long for me to land an interview. At least I had my boyfriend, Baron, to help with my portion of the bills.

I was so engrossed in my job search that I hadn't noticed Baron walk into our bedroom. "Don't even trip, baby. You gon' be straight. I will have some money next week if this partnership goes through," Baron assured, kissing my lips.

Baron and I had been together for over a year, and honestly, I wasn't sure where things were going. For the longest, I felt like he thought I was a hoe because I let him fuck on the first night. It was my third month working in the strip club, and I was still mourning my mother's death and needed a release. I wasn't shy. I knew I wanted to fuck him the minute we locked eyes. He wasn't necessarily my type, but his deep-sea waves instantly made my pussy wet.

Being the confident, thick girl I was, I sauntered right over to him and started bouncing my ass on his dick like we knew each other. I didn't even have to hit the stage. Baron kept me in his lap. As the money piled up, Baron kept the drinks flowing. That night, he took me back to his house, and we'd been together ever since.

Things weren't bad between us. Sometimes I just wondered if there was something more out there. We never discussed kids or marriage because those things didn't seem attainable. Hell, I wasn't even sure I wanted that. Baron never spoke of it, so neither did I.

"I know, baby, but I enjoy having my own money. You know that."

Baron was a mechanic. He had his car shop but was still somewhat in the streets. I didn't have to worry about him being gone all night making plays because he sold his weed in large quantities. His love for cars outweighed his love for the streets, which allowed us plenty of time to spend together. While he paid most of the bills, I handled the groceries and utilities, and I was okay with that. Now that I was no longer working, everything would fall on him.

"Yeah, I been telling yo' ass to quit that job for months. Ain't no rush on finding another one. I'll make sure you get everything you need. We good."

I heard him loud and clear, but I still had my doubts. I had never been the type to depend on people. Let alone a man. Baron hadn't given a reason to make me think he wouldn't keep his word. It wasn't like I spent lots of money anyway.

"Royce wants me to come work at the salon, but I don't know. Doing hair hasn't been my favorite hobby as of late." I had no intention of working there. My car getting fixed was my primary concern.

"Nah, man, fuck you need to work up in that shop for? I'm not with all them niggas that be in there," he chided.

"It's also a barber shop, Baron. If I went to work in the shop, it would be to save some extra money."

"Chi, this is my last time telling yo' ass I got—"

"I know you got me," I repeated. "What if I wanna do something special for you, baby?" I cooed, wrapping my arms around his neck.

"Just lay low for a minute. Let's see how things work out like this. A nigga trying to take care of yo' ass, and you won't let 'em," he said as his phone buzzed in his pocket. "This Byron. I'm bouta head up to the shop. He just dropped your car off," he stated.

Byron was Baron's younger brother, who he desperately tried to keep out of the streets. He went to great lengths to make sure of it too. Against his parent's wishes, Baron fronted Byron the money to start his own tow trucking business. His parents disagreed because they felt Byron was a grown man who needed to care for himself. Honestly, if I were him, I would've done the same thing. Keeping Byron out of the streets was more important than proving a point.

Baron's parents were old school. Since Byron had been in jail several times, they wasted no time throwing him out the minute he graduated high school. He didn't choose the college or trade route, so he had no option but to come live with us. For months, Baron didn't speak to his parents. He didn't understand how they could be so hard on their son. Baron didn't have that issue because he picked up a trade. His mother, Mrs. Janice, doted on Baron. To me, it was sickening to watch. Baron was the golden child, and Byron was the fuck up.

"What do you think is wrong with it?" I quizzed. The car

stopping in the middle of the road had been terrifying. Luckily, Baron wasn't far and came to pick me up.

"I won't know until I look at it," he replied, grabbing his blunt out of the ashtray. He kissed my lips and told me he would call me with the diagnostics.

I prayed it was nothing major because I needed my car. Uber was expensive in Atlanta, and I didn't want to depend on Baron and Royce to take me everywhere. Now that my car was down, I had to figure out what I would do with my time. I didn't want to get in the habit of lounging around; that had never been me. It was only Monday, so I had a long week ahead. Instead of lounging around, I decided to cook dinner. What better way to make my man happy than to cook his favorite meal?

# Chapter 2
## *Baron*

"Nigga, what the fuck I tell you about fuckin' with the female customers? That shit is bad for business, bruh." I shook my head.

Nicole, one of my regular customers, had just left the shop. Byron was still young, so it was natural for him to want to fuck all the hoes. I was cool with that. He was a grown-ass man. When it came to my business, though, I didn't like that shit. It would be different if bitches knew how to play their position. Byron was fucking the hoes who wanted to be in their feelings. Showing up to the shop and shit, disrupting my place of business.

"Ain't shit. I was only asking the hoe how her day was going," he shot back once she was out of earshot.

I ain't gon' lie, Nicole was fine as hell, and even though I thought about fucking her, I let Byron hop on her. He needed an older bitch who could teach his ass a thing or two.

"Nigga, I saw her slide you the number. What you gon' do with all that ass?"

"Fuck you mean, nigga? I'ma be balls deep in her shit. She

older, so I know that lil' pussy got some power to it." He laughed, dapping me up.

Byron was six years younger than me, but that never stopped us from being close. I used to be more to myself, but I saw how my parents treated Byron once he started running the streets. The first time Byron was caught selling weed in school and expelled, Mama was ready to send his ass off to boarding school. Had it not been for me convincing her to enroll him in an alternative school in the city, he would've been shipped off.

My father tried to be hard on him, but it only made Byron rebel. The older he got, the more trouble he found. If anybody ever asked, I told them Byron only got in trouble one time, but that shit was for appearances. The truth was, Byron had been getting into trouble since he was thirteen, from vandalizing property to breaking and entering. You name it, Byron did it. The only thing he hadn't done was murk a nigga.

My father, Bernard, was a judge. Keeping Byron's behavior under wraps was vital to him. Now that Byron was over eighteen, it was hard to hide his adult record. Whether Byron recognized it or not, his poor decisions could cost our father his career. Especially since he had one of his colleagues sign off on sealed documents for Byron. For that alone, my parents wanted nothing to do with him. That was where I stepped in.

When Byron graduated, they thought kicking him out was a good idea, knowing he had nowhere to go. Instead of watching my brother get tossed out on the streets, I let his ass stay with me. Chi didn't mind, either. That's why I fucked with her. She was loyal and kept me grounded. Plus, she and Byron got along.

"Yeah, right. You bouta head to the crib?"

"I'm bouta slide down the block real quick. See wasup with my nigga Bean."

Byron already knew my position when it came to Bean. I

ain't fuck with that nigga because he was always turning Byron on to some other shit. I'd known Bean since he was a lil' nigga running around terrorizing the neighborhood. When Byron started hanging around him, I already knew what time it was. Trouble. Byron swore up and down Bean wasn't a bad influence. His lengthy record proved otherwise.

"Man, why the fuck yo' ass keep hanging around that nigga? I thought we had an agreement. The last thing you need is to catch another case," I scolded.

We agreed that I would front the money to help him start and get his business off the ground, and he would stay out of trouble. Byron wasn't getting off to a good start.

It was bad enough that our parents had disowned him. Shit, I was still trying to figure out how to deal with that. Until now, we had never been a divided family. I was the only one trying to make shit right, but I didn't know what else to tell him. I was done trying if Byron couldn't meet me halfway and get his act together. I was his big brother, not his babysitter. I couldn't want it more than he wanted it for himself.

"Aye, man, get yo' panties out of a bunch, nigga. I ain't on shit. I'm gon' shoot some dice. Take all them niggas' money and shit. You know how I do." Byron laughed.

This nigga thought shit was funny. I was tired of trying to keep this nigga on the straight and narrow. I didn't understand what was so hard about making your money legally, coming home to a cooked meal, and getting yo' dick sucked. What the fuck more could a man ask for? I needed to find this nigga a girlfriend. Byron didn't have issues getting bitches. The problem was, he only fucked with strippers and lil' ass girls who had nothing to offer but wet pussy.

"Nah, I'm just saying. You need to start thinking more about your future and how you gon' elevate your new business," I advised.

"Nigga, here you go preaching, sounding like Bernard's ol' uptight ass. I'm good. I ain't trying to hear none of that shit," Byron stated, dismissively waving me off. He hopped into his truck and sped off.

Once Byron was gone, I popped the hood of Chi's car. I needed to see what could've gone wrong between now and her last oil change. Hopefully, it was something minor that wouldn't take long to fix. Even if it did, I wasn't in a rush for her to be driving. Chi needed to sit her ass down somewhere anyway. If she wasn't at work, she was out hanging with Royce. Going out now and again was acceptable, but this bitch stayed on Chi's line, wanting to go out every other day. If she wasn't Chi's cousin, I would think she wanted to fuck my bitch. I had been thinking about putting a baby in her ass anyway. Still, I was skeptical because she never talked about having kids. I never brought it up, so she probably thought I didn't want to have any.

After running the diagnostics, I determined that Chi's transmission had gone out, which would take thousands to replace. Luckily, I had discounts on parts, so it would only be half the cost since she didn't have to pay for labor. Pulling out my phone, I dialed Chi's number.

"Hey baby, is it bad? What's wrong with my car?" she anxiously asked. The panic in her voice caused me to chuckle. "Why you laughing, Baron? What's wrong with Nissy?"

I didn't understand the logic behind females naming their cars, but every bitch who came into my shop had a name for their vehicle. Chi was no different. I LAUGHED when I met her and learned she'd named her Nissan Altima Nissy. It had to be the dumbest shit I'd ever heard. Once I started asking customers what name they had given to their cars, they would state it with no hesitation. One nigga even told me he named his truck Black Thunder and winked when he said the shit. I almost beat that nigga with a tire iron. I wasn't with none of that gay ass shit.

"Transmission went out. I got it covered, though."

Working on cars was something I had been interested in since I was younger. I could take a whole car apart and build that bitch back up. Instead of going the traditional college route, I chose a vocational school to learn about cars. It was a waste of time and money other than getting a certification. Half the shit they taught, I already knew. Bernard wasn't pleased with my decision but was content as long as I was doing something with my life. I never saw myself in the same line of work as my father. It just wasn't in me. Something about punishing a nigga 'cus he had to feed his family was crazy. I ain't want no parts in that shit.

"How long is that going to take? I can't be without a car, Baron."

Chi was a woman who knew exactly what she wanted. Sometimes, she was too strong-willed, which caused us to bump heads. Chi acted like me being the man and wearing the pants in the relationship was a problem. Like now, I wanted her to stay at home and relax for a few months, but she kept talking about finding another job. Then, Royce called her on that bullshit about coming to work at the shop. My bitch wasn't going anywhere near that place if I had anything to do with it. Too many niggas ran in and out of that bitch. Plus, it was dead smack in the middle of the hood. Chi failed to realize there were plenty of bitches who would kill to be in her position. Yet, she wanted to do the opposite.

"Shit, a few weeks. A month maybe. It depends on my workload." There was a long pause before she sighed heavily.

"Well, I cooked some baked ziti for dinner. I put you and Byron's plates in the microwave."

Chi knew the way to a nigga's heart, and she could throw

down in the kitchen. That lil' extra weight she carried didn't bother me. I loved that shit. Chi was thick in all the right places. That lil' fupa gave me something to hold onto while I was hitting her shit from the back. She was confident too. I peeped that the night I met her. Chi was the thickest bitch in the club, but she didn't let that stop her from approaching me and getting a bag. Chi let me fuck the same night I met her, which made me wonder how many other niggas she had done that shit with.

"Aight, let me finish this paperwork so I can close up shop," I told her, ending our call.

After switching the open sign off, I locked the front door. Once I hit the automatic button to close the garage, that was it for the day. I had to ensure the shop was in order before heading to my office to send invoices to my customers. Once I finished emailing about a transmission, my phone buzzed again.

"Sup, ma dukes?"

"Boy, you better act like you got some sense when I call. You sound like your brother. A hoodlum," she snapped.

I did my best to stifle the laughter that threatened to erupt. Mama would punch me in the back of my head if she thought I took her for a joke. If nothing else, Mama didn't play that hood shit. She always told us that when we were in her presence, we would talk like we had some sense. That was one reason Mama didn't like Chi. She felt like she was too ghetto for me. Yes, Chi was a lil' ghetto, but she had an off switch when needed. I explained how smart Chi was, but that didn't change her perspective.

"You right. My fault."

"You should come around here and grab a plate. I cooked neck bones, cabbage, and macaroni and cheese with some of those yeast dinner rolls y'all like. I also made a caramel cake. You know how your father is. He has to have his caramel cake once a month, even though his doctor keeps telling him he's not supposed to eat sweets." She chuckled.

My mouth salivated upon hearing her read off the menu. Janice was easily one of the best cooks in Atlanta. She used to have a food truck but closed it down after getting sick. Mama was a breast cancer survivor and was grateful to have lived, so she decided taking it easy would be the best thing to do. That didn't stop her from throwing down at home, though. She called me at least four times a week to get a plate. I told her I'd be on the way after finishing my paperwork and ended the call. I texted Chi to let her know I was stopping by my parent's house before coming home.

Before making it to my parent's house, I stopped at the gas station to fill up my tank. I hated stopping at the gas stations in the hood because somebody always had their hand out, asking for money. That shit bothered a nigga because I felt like we all had the same twenty-four hours in a day, and I wasn't giving away my hard-earned money to the next mothafucka. When I pulled up to the pump, I noticed a bad lil' brown skin chick with a short haircut hop out of a Mercedes Benz.

As if she felt me watching her, she turned her head in the direction of my car. My windows were heavily tinted, so I wasn't worried about her catching my intense gaze. I put out the blunt that I'd been smoking and turned off the ignition. Shawty damn near looked familiar, but I couldn't place it. She could've been a customer, but I'd remember if I had seen her pretty ass. Once inside, I stood behind her as she paid for her gas. I started to pay for it, but a nigga ain't want to seem thirsty. When she turned around to leave, she glanced in my direction.

"Baron, is that you?" she quizzed, stopping in her tracks.

*Damn, she knows my name?* I walked in her direction to get a closer look at her face.

"Taina? Damn, wasup witchu' ma?" I greeted, pulling her in for a hug.

Our embrace lasted longer than I intended, but she smelled good enough to eat. Taina was my ex. We had a lengthy history that ended abruptly. We had dated off and on for five years before I met Chi. Taina looked better than I remembered. She'd chopped off her long hair and traded it in for a pixie cut. I ain't gon' lie; that shit was sexy as fuck.

"It's so good to see you, Bear." She blushed, calling me by the nickname she'd given me back in high school.

Taina and I had always had a thing for each other but didn't start dating until our adult years due to her going into the military.

"I see you still looking good, T."

She smiled as she did a full spin, so I could get a better glimpse of her slim-thick physique. Taina had always been fit, but her hips had filled out a little more since the last time we saw each other. Her titties were on full display and sat up perfectly. My eyes lustfully roamed her body as I liked my lips. My dick got hard thinking about all the ways I used to flip her lil' ass around.

"Wow, out of all people, I can't believe I ran into you. How have you been?"

I opened the door and allowed her to walk out in front of me, so I could get a good look at her round ass. Once we made it to her car, I started pumping her gas. After telling her about my shop, we briefly caught up on each other's lives. I was surprised to learn that she had recently had a baby and had moved back to Atlanta. One of the reasons we'd broken up was because Taina wanted to move to Dubai. That didn't align with my plans, and I wasn't willing to compromise, which resulted in us calling it quits. The love we had between us had never ceased. I pulled out my phone to check the time and realized I needed to get going before Mama started calling and asking where I was. Standing there talking to Taina brought back memories.

"Shit, it was nice seeing you, but I gotta get to Mama's before she calls, cussing my ass out." I grinned.

Taina grabbed my hand while tilting her head to the side. Like always, her dimpled smile drew me in. I pulled her in for another hug. This time, we rocked from side to side. Our chemistry was evident, and I needed to leave before I did something I would regret later.

"Put my number in your phone. We gotta hang out sometimes." I hesitated before handing her my phone so I could lock her number in. I knew I was treading in dangerous territory, but there was no harm in catching up. "What's wrong, Bear? You gotta a girlfriend or something?"

Nodding my head, I grabbed my phone from her and placed it back in my pocket.

"Listen, I'ma hit you up, ma."

"We're just old friends catching up, right?" She smiled.

"Yeah, man. I'ma lock you in. Make sure you answer when I call too." I jogged to my car and hopped in.

After she drove off, I realized that I never pumped my gas. Fucking around with Taina was going to lead me into a world of trouble if I wasn't careful. I'd cheated on Chi several times before. However, it was nothing more than me getting my dick wet. With Taina, I had to tread lightly.

"Took you long enough, son. Come in here and sit down, so you can eat. Let me warm your plate up." Mama greeted me when I walked into the foyer.

As always, she kept the house spotless and smelling good. I couldn't remember the last time anything was out of place in the home we'd grown up in. We had always lived in the suburbs. How Byron managed to get introduced to the street life was a mystery to me. He claimed a hood he never even grew up in. The shit was lame as fuck.

"Where's Bernard?" I quizzed, peering around the corner.

"Your dad went to go watch the game at the Gates estate," she replied, referring to the neighbors on the next street over.

Due to my father being a high-ranking judge, they lived in a gated community that was heavily secured. There had been multiple occasions where people threatened to murder our entire family simply because they disagreed with their sentence. I didn't understand that shit.

Mama pulled the plate from the microwave and set it on the table with a napkin and a cold Sprite.

"I was coming to grab a plate for me and Chi."

With a raised brow, she glared in my direction disapprovingly. "Who? Oh no, baby, I only made enough for us. I packed some up for your dad to take to work tomorrow. I saved just enough so you could have a plate."

I remembered Chi telling me she cooked, but this food smelled good as fuck. On top of that, my stomach was growling because I hadn't eaten shit all day. You couldn't tell a woman from the South that you would eat her food later. Mama considered that shit rude. I picked up my fork and dug in while Mama rambled about the women in her book club.

"What's that nappy-headed brother of yours been up to? I'm sure he's out there gangbanging."

Even though it was hard getting Byron to clean up his act, I still felt like my parents were too harsh on him. It was morally wrong if it didn't align with my father's core values. Shit, I wasn't exempt from his wrath either. It took months to convince them to let me attend a vocational school. Bernard thought a college education was the only answer. I knew differently. We live in the age of social media, and hundreds of thousands of people get rich by creating content. They would think the worst of me if they knew I was selling weed on the side. Byron knew but never said anything. That's why I would always have his back.

"He good. I had him go pick up Chi's car off the highway. He's been working on advertising and marketing his business to attract new customers," I lied, knowing damn well that nigga wasn't doing shit but waiting for me to call him with the next job.

All his jobs came from my customers. I was cool with that, but I knew Byron had the potential to expand his business. It didn't matter how much I stayed on him; Byron would do whatever he wanted to spite our parents.

"I can't believe he doesn't want more out of his life. I swear, I went wrong somewhere with that boy. We didn't have these problems out of you."

I didn't mind spending time at my parent's house, but when it turned into a Byron bashing session, that was my cue to leave. She had something negative to say for every positive thing I said about him. Little did she know, that shit was draining and toxic. I quickly finished my plate and told my mother I would call to check up on her the following day. I was ready to get home and chill with Chi.

It took less than thirty minutes to make it home to our apartment in Riverdale. When I walked through the door, the aroma of baked ziti invaded my nostrils. Chi was sitting on the couch watching TV. Once she noticed me, she stood up and stretched, showing off her voluptuous frame. Wrapping my arms around her, I planted a soft kiss on her neck.

"Umm," she moaned. "You ready to eat?"

"Yeah, you." Grinning, I licked my lips.

"I'm talking about your food, crazy. There's some garlic bread to go along with it as well."

"Damn, I'm not that hungry right now," I explained, attempting to wrap my arms back around her.

Chi stepped back and put her hand up between us. "Wait, so you ate dinner at your mom's?"

She caught a nigga red-handed. There was nothing I could say.

"I'ma still eat the food you made, baby, just not right now."

That look was all too familiar. Rage consumed Chi as she stormed off to the kitchen. Following closely behind, I watched as she pulled my plate out of the microwave and tossed it in the trash. If that wasn't dramatic enough, she pulled the baked ziti out of the oven and threw the entire glass pan in the trash. After she finished that, she hurled the breadsticks in my direction one by one.

"Aye, man, the fuck is you trippin' for?"

"Nigga, fuck you. This is the last time I go out of my fucking way to make a meal for yo' goofy ass, and you come in here talking about you just ate at yo' mama's house! The fuck do I look like to you, Baron? A housewife? Ain't no ring on my finger, and even if it was, this shit is unacceptable. Over the last month, you've done this shit at least ten fucking times. What's wrong? You don't know how to tell Janice's ass, no? What, you scared she gon' disown you like she did Byron?"

My chances of getting some pussy tonight had gone down the drain. Chi was mad, and I knew it would take her a minute to calm her crazy ass down. Chi was sweet but had this explosive angry side that I didn't like.

"Chill out with all that, Chi. Damn, you act like a nigga said he wasn't gon' eat yo' food."

"Baron, I made baked ziti because you fucking asked for it, and I know it's your favorite. Even though I know how to cook it, I still have the recipe from yo' overbearing ass mama and used hers. You be over there so much, you might as well move the fuck in. Shit, Byron be here more than yo' ass."

Now her ass was tripping foreal. I only went over there a few times throughout the week. It wasn't my fault she cooked every day. Chi was being unreasonable; she knew I made sure to spend time with Mama due to her having breast cancer. Even though she'd been in remission for ten years, you never knew if or when it'd reappear.

"Look, I already told you what it is. It ain't my fault my mama is here, and yours ain't," I shot back but instantly regretted it.

Shock and bewilderment flashed across her face. "Oh, you a dirty mothafucka. How could you say something so mean, Baron? You can get your shit and stay with ya' mammy. How you a grown-ass man hiding the fact that you sell weed? It's probably because you don't want them to view you like Byron. It would kill you to be labeled as the fuck up. I don't want to be with a nigga who won't unlatch from his mama's titty. Grow the fuck up, titty boy! You ain't right for how you allow them to think the worst of that boy when you be doing fucked up shit too!" she screamed, slamming the bedroom door.

I ain't gon' lie; her saying that fucked me up, but I deserved it. Instead of fueling her fire, I decided to apologize. Surprisingly, she didn't lock the door behind her. When I entered the room, Chi was sitting on the bed, hyperventilating with a tear-soaked face. This wasn't the first time I'd witnessed her like that. I sat on the bed beside her and waited until she calmed down. I didn't know how to help, so I rubbed the small of her back.

"Baby, I'm sorry. I didn't mean it like that," I pleaded. The hurt in her eyes was evident.

"Get your hands off me, Baron. I'm fine." She sneered,

shoving my hand away. "I think you should sleep on the couch."

"Can we just talk about this?"

Chi stood up and tossed two pillows in my direction.

Fuck it. If the bitch didn't want to talk, I wasn't going to force her. I hated how she tried to blame everything on me. Her ass was tripping about some food for no reason. I ate over at Mama's house; shit wasn't even that deep. This shit was starting to get old. Now that she was no longer working, I expected a hot meal every day after work. I didn't care if I ate at my Mama's house. At least I could take lunch to work the next day.

Grabbing both pillows off the bed, I pulled a sheet out of the linen closet and placed it on the couch. Turning on ESPN, I tried to catch the game's highlights before falling asleep. Not long after, I heard Byron come in and go straight to the kitchen.

"Damn, what happened to the food?"

"Ask your stupid ass, brother!" Chi yelled from the bedroom.

Byron shook his head and grabbed a bag of chips before heading to his room.

* * *

"Do you have the part to my car yet, Baron?"

Two weeks had passed since I received the part for Chi's car. I wasn't telling her ass that. Royce kept calling her with that bullshit, inviting her out every chance she got. I knew Chi would decline because she didn't like driving places with other people. She preferred her car, so she could leave on her own terms and not have to wait until the next person was ready to leave.

"I told you I would let you know."

"It's already been over two weeks. It shouldn't take that long to get a part."

There I was, trying to make shit easier for Chi, and all she kept doing was complaining. I had the perfect system for us, and she acted like a defiant little girl. Chi was down to earth, but she spoke her mind a little too much, and I felt like this was the only way to get her to respect me more.

A few months ago, we got into this big argument about Chi respecting how I felt about her hanging out with Royce. She felt she could do whatever she wanted since we weren't married. I went to my father for advice because I wasn't sure what to do. I'd thought about marriage in the past, but not with Chi. My mother was right. Chi was rough around the edges, but I knew the real Chi. She was down for a nigga and had been since we met. She was one of the funniest women I'd ever dated. I tried to get her to enroll in some college courses, but she refused.

My father told me the problem was me allowing her to pay bills. In his opinion, as the man, I was the provider, and Chi shouldn't have been working. Now that I'd taken his advice and tried to take control, it had backfired on me. Her ass was walking around with this stank attitude, like a mothafucka owed her something.

"You want me to go to the manufacturer and make the part myself?" Chi folded her arms across her chest while shifting her weight to one leg.

"Do what you gotta do."

That was the shit I was talking about. Her smart-ass mouth made me want to choke the shit out of her.

"I'll just call around and look for the part myself."

Not wanting to hear her mouth, I grabbed my phone off the charger and left the house. I was part of the problem, but there was a method to my madness. Once I made it to my car, I pulled out my phone and called Taina. I wasn't on shit; I just needed some company while I had a drink at the bar. Chi was getting on my nerves. She needed time to cool down before I returned because if I stayed there any longer, shit was gon' get ugly.

# Chapter 3
## *Chi*

"Chicago Parker," the nurse called.

I hated going to the hospital. Being there always brought back terrible memories. I remember the last time I got a call from a hospital because Charae had overdosed. Now that she was gone, the feeling had intensified. I remember having to drive almost eleven hours just to identify her body. The memory would forever be etched in my brain. It was crazy how fast life could pass you by. People think they have all the time in the world to change, but that wasn't the reality I lived in. I knew I needed to get my shit together.

"Hi, my name is Taina. I'm going to be your nurse. What brings you in today?" she asked while taking my vitals.

I couldn't help but notice how beautiful she was. Her short pixie cut looked good, but I knew Royce could do it better. I started to give her Royce's information but didn't want to offend her. Besides, I wasn't there for all of that.

After I explained my symptoms, she made me pee in a cup and advised me that a doctor would be in to see me soon. I had been throwing up for days and couldn't keep anything down. Baron and I had sushi a few days prior, and I was almost certain that was what made me sick. It was my first time trying raw sushi, and it would be my last. It sucked because Baron was trying to get me out of the house by taking me on a date. I had gotten all dressed up, only to be locked in the bathroom, hurling over the toilet.

For the past few weeks, I had been in a funk and didn't want to do much of anything. Since I didn't have a car or job, I had slipped into a dark space that I was trying hard to get out of. Royce kept trying to get me to hang out. Since Alex was working a lot more, she had a lot of time on her hands. Most times, I declined just to keep the peace between Baron and me. I had set up a few interviews in hopes that my car would be fixed, with no luck. Every week, Baron kept promising that he would have it fixed. I hoped he wasn't lying just so I wouldn't leave. Feeling like a prisoner in your own house was enough to make anybody go crazy.

"Hello, Ms. Parker. My name is Dr. Yancy. I hear you can't keep anything down."

"I think I got food poisoning. I ate raw sushi a few days ago."

Dr. Yancy had me lean back on the bed while she pressed on each side of my stomach. When she was done, she sat on a stool and rolled over to the computer to pull up my chart. Even though I was slightly overweight, I was still healthy.

"Okay, so we have two things going on. The first is that your blood pressure is slightly elevated. The second is that you probably had a bad reaction to the sushi because you're pregnant."

My eyes fluttered as I opened then closed my mouth, attempting to protest. The words were there; I just couldn't get them past the lump in my throat. This bitch was a liar. There was no way on God's green earth that I was pregnant. From what I'd been told, it was medically impossible. All I could think about was the countless times I'd allowed Baron to shoot up the club. I regretted not taking those back shots instead.

"Ms. Parker, are you okay?"

I hadn't realized my breathing had become rapid. I was trying to catch my breath but was overwhelmed with emotion. I wasn't ready for a baby.

"My chest is really tight!" I cried.

Dr. Yancy instructed me to take a few deep breaths. Her hand rested on my shoulder as she did the breathing exercises with me. I didn't want to bring a baby into this fucked up world. My life wasn't the worst, but it damn sure wasn't the best. I struggled daily to get out of bed, and most days, I was sad. People thought I was fine, but on the inside, I battled with depression. That wasn't the type of mother I wanted to be for my child.

"That's impossible. I can't be pregnant."

"Why do you say it's impossible? Have you had some sort of medical testing to prove that?"

"Yes, about three years ago," I told her.

My breathing returned to normal as Dr. Yancy questioned me about how often I had panic attacks. I had them every other day, but I wasn't going to tell her ass that. The first thing doctors did was try to put you on a bunch of medication, and I wasn't going for that.

"Okay. I want to do an ultrasound to get a better look at your cervix. Sit tight. We'll have a technician come down shortly."

Shortly turned into three hours. Once the ultrasound technician was done, Dr. Yancy came back to explain that everything looked fine and I shouldn't have a problem carrying the baby full term. That news was devastating, but it explained so much. I'd been sleeping a lot, and lately, I'd been nauseous. After waiting another thirty minutes, Taina came back into the room to give me my prescriptions.

"Congratulations. I hope you have a happy and healthy pregnancy. Becoming a mother has been the most fulfilling experience. I wouldn't trade it for the world." She beamed with excitement. "Dr. Yancy wants you to get some prenatal vitamins. You can purchase them at your local drug store," she explained, like I was stupid.

I wasn't in the mood for her chipper ass. Maybe I was jealous because I felt like the world was closing in on me. Whatever the reason, I was ready to get the fuck out of that hospital.

I snatched the prescription out of her hand. "Whatever."

"Excuse me?"

I didn't even bother to turn around because I knew I was out of line. She hadn't done anything wrong, but I wasn't trying to hear none of that. I didn't care to hear about her experience with motherhood or how much she enjoyed it. She could tell that shit to the next pregnant bitch.

By the time I made it home, Byron was asleep on the couch. It pissed me off because he had a whole bedroom to sleep in. There was a plate on the floor, along with a cup. He had even smoked a blunt and left the tobacco from the cigarillo on the table. I'd just cleaned up the house this morning, and now it looked like I hadn't touched it.

Instead of waking him up, I called Baron and told him to get his ass home. If he didn't talk to his brother, we were going to have a problem. I couldn't keep living like this. After I got off the phone with Baron, I went upstairs and took a bubble bath. Once I was relaxed, I called Royce. I couldn't keep secrets from her, and if I tried, she had her ways of finding out.

"You're what?" Royce shrieked into the phone.

I hated for her excitement to be short lived because I wasn't sure what I wanted to do. Just thinking about having a baby gave me terrible anxiety.

"You heard me right. I'm about eight weeks. I have to follow up with my doctor."

"I'm so excited for you. What did Baron say?"

"He doesn't know. I'm not sure if I wanna go through with this, Royce. I'm not fit to be a mother yet."

Now that I think about it, I'd never even held a newborn baby before. I didn't know the first thing to do with a baby. What if I dropped it? Then people would be looking at me like I was crazy.

"Chi, you are going to be a great mother. You need to tell Baron, so he can help support you through this. Just don't make any decisions until you talk to him about it first."

"I'll take a few weeks to rest on it. Baron already has me sitting in this house like I'm a fucking housewife or some shit. He wants me to stay home and cook and clean after him and his trifling ass brother, and I'm not doing that. He doesn't know, but I recently looked at his bank statement, and he's barely making ends meet at the shop. Bringing a baby into a struggle doesn't seem smart."

"Wait, so he doesn't want you to work but can barely maintain his shop? Girl, you better watch out. You know how niggas be on power trips. Still, I want you to think about it. I know you were told that you couldn't have kids. This could be your miracle baby."

Royce had some valid points. However, this was something I hadn't prepared myself for. Having a child was a big responsibility, and I could barely take care of my damn self. I was twenty-four years old with no real goals. Being pregnant only made me realize I needed to do better. I'd never been the type to become complacent.

"Yeah, you're right."

"I know. Just weigh out all the options. I'll support you on whatever you decide." Royce was more than my cousin. She was my sister, and I couldn't imagine life without her.

"Well, let me get out of this tub, so I can go to bed," I said and ended our call.

Once I was done taking a bath, I oiled my body down with some coconut oil. After oiling my scalp, I put my hair in two french braids, so I could wear it in its natural state.

"Sup' bae?" Baron said, coming into the bathroom.

"Hey, baby," I replied and kissed him on the lips. Even though Baron had me fucked up, I still missed him. He had been keeping the shop open later to make extra money.

"Damn, you smell good. C'mere."

Wrapping my arms around his neck, Baron lifted me onto the sink. We kissed passionately as his hands freely roamed my naked body. He slipped his fingers into my wetness while kissing my neck. My pussy was already wet, but being pregnant had me even wetter. Hopefully, Baron wouldn't notice the difference and start asking questions. If he did, I was prepared to lie like my life depended on it. I didn't want him to know about this pregnancy just yet.

"That pussy wet for me, baby."

"Um, yes," I purred into his ear.

Baron unbuckled his pants and let them drop to his ankles. He pulled his dick out and ran it up and down my clit. By that time, I was practically begging him to stick it in. I had some pent-up frustrations and wanted to ride his dick until I couldn't take it. Baron's sex was wonderful, but I might have been too much of a freak for him. I liked to be slutted out from time to time. If I wanted to be fucked like that, I had to get him drunk.

"You ready for this dick?" he whispered in my ear before filling me up with all nine inches.

Gasping, I wrapped my legs around his waist as he slowly drilled into me. All I could hear were our moans and heavy breathing. I grabbed his face and kissed him while slipping a little tongue to intensify the moment. I felt myself on the verge of an orgasm. My pussy muscles tightened around him as my nails dug into his back.

"Ah shit, baby. I'm about to cum," I announced, burying my head into his chest.

"Yeah, cum all over this dick, ma. This yo' shit."

"Fuck!" I shrieked as I reached my climax. Baron had a bitch seeing stars.

"Nah, don't get tired now," he said as he picked up the pace.

I didn't care who heard me. I needed this release. Baron's dick started pulsating as he came inside me. When we were done, he helped me off the sink and turned on the shower. We took a shower together and fell asleep shortly after.

The next day, Baron was up and dressed by seven.

"Good morning." I smiled, stretching my arms outward.

"Good morning, beautiful. You looked like you were sleeping so peacefully. I didn't want to wake you."

"No, it's okay. I wanted to ask you if I could drop you off at work and keep the car, so I can run some errands."

Baron hesitated, which only irritated me.

"You know what? Never mind. I'll see if Royce can let me use her car."

"Damn, why you tripping, Chi? I told you I need to fix the brakes. How I look having my woman riding around like that? The shop has been busy, so I haven't had time to fix them yet, baby."

Little did Baron know, I was on to his bullshit. I wasn't

stupid. There wasn't a mechanic on this earth who would drive around on bad brakes, knowing it could ruin the entire brake system. I was no expert, but I knew a little something.

"It's cool. Like I said, I'll ask Royce since my man can't do it," I shot back.

"Here. I'll Cash App you some money to pay for an Uber. How much you need?"

"Not a damn dime. You can keep your money, Baron. I won't ask to use your car anymore," I said and slammed the bathroom door.

Once I heard the front door close, I went downstairs to the kitchen and cooked a light breakfast. After I was done eating, I cleaned up the kitchen and threw a load of clothes into the washer. Byron's big, overgrown ass kept leaving his dirty clothes on top of the dryer, and I refused to touch them. Instead, I left them there for him.

An hour later, I was dressed and inside an Uber on my way to the grocery store. Since Baron kept eating at his mother's house, I wasn't cooking anything. I wanted to lose a few pounds, so meal-prepping was the best option.

"Chi? Is that you?" a familiar voice said from behind me.

I quickly turned around and stared into the face of my former college roommate, Demi. Our friendship hadn't ended on the best terms. Nonetheless, she was still someone who I considered a friend. When I left Tilman, we lost touch and hadn't seen each other until now.

"Demi, you look good, girl."

Demi had smooth, dark skin with red undertones. She was gorgeous, to say the least. She was still slim, but her hips and thighs had filled out, giving her a curvier look. Back when we were in college, Demi was built straight up and down. She always joked about how she looked like a little boy since she barely had titties.

"Thanks, so do you. It's been what, three years since we last saw each other?"

"Girl, yes. We fell out about Dion," I reminded her, rolling my eyes. Looking at her cart, I saw several cans of infant formula.

Demi followed my gaze and nervously laughed.

"We sure did. I wish I would've listened to you then. Now I'm stuck dealing with this mothafucka for the next eighteen years," she revealed.

"Are you serious? Y'all been messing around all this time? I'm not judging you, but he is a piece of work," I recalled.

I didn't want to go back to that place. The way I'd been expelled made me dislike everything about that school. My hopes and dreams had been taken from me in a split second, and that shook me to my core.

"Yes, girl. I'll have to tell you about that another time. Do you live in the area?"

"I do. I live in the apartments close to the highway."

"That's crazy. I live a few streets over. What were the odds of us running into each other? What are you doing when you leave here? I was going to get a seafood boil at that new place they just opened across the street."

That was where she lost me. Usually, I loved eating seafood, but lately, it had been making me sick, so I would have to pass on that. Witnessing the look on my face, Demi asked if there was something else in the area I would eat. We decided on a local brunch spot located in the same plaza as the grocery store. We grocery shopped together while briefly catching up. I couldn't believe Demi was still dealing with Dion's scandalous ass. After lunch, Demi and I exchanged numbers and promised to link up soon.

I got in an Uber and went all the way across town to pay Tracy a visit. I hadn't seen her in a while, and I was certain the bitch was going to shit bricks once I showed up on her doorstep. My father and I weren't on speaking terms, but he did write me from time to time. It was good to know he thought of me. However, I couldn't bring myself to relive past traumas, so I chose not to communicate with him.

The Uber pulled up to Tracy's house within thirty minutes. Everything was just as I remembered. The yard had been freshly manicured, and the bushes that lined the walkway to the door were neatly trimmed. I could tell there had been some work done on the outside of the house, and it looked great.

As I walked up the driveway, Tracy came scrambling outside with her robe on. Her skin was flushed, and from the way her hair was disheveled, I could tell she'd just had sex.

"Chi, you don't just show up to people's house unannounced. Can I help you?" Her voice was prim and proper.

"Girl, cut the shit. You know why I'm here," I replied as I walked up on her. "Are you going to let me in?"

Tracy's eyes darted to the door as if someone was on the other side watching. "No, I'm not. What do you want?" Her voice had risen an octave as she blocked the doorway.

"I just wanted to ask you a question. The day I got expelled from Tilman, how did you find out so fast?"

All the color drained from Tracy's face. Struggling to find her words, she started backing up until she reached the front door. Tracy thought she was slick. She had gotten away with her conniving ways for far too long. Somebody had to put a stop to her shit, and I was the perfect match for the job. This was personal.

"I-I don't know what you're talking about," she stammered.

"Bitch, yes, you do. Keep playing crazy, and I'll whoop your ass all up and down this driveway," I fumed.

I could feel myself getting angrier by the second.

"Chicago, I swear I didn't know about it."

"Oh, really? Then why were you on the campus? I don't recall Arrington going to college. You know what? Don't even worry about answering that question because if you lie to me again, I'm going to spazz. Just understand one thing. I know you fuck with Dion Walker. And you know what's so sad? You and your hoe ass daughter are so jealous of me that you started fucking the dean to make sure I got expelled." I laughed.

"You don't have proof of that," she confidently shot back.

"Oh, but I do, ma'am. Try me if you want to, and this pretty little house of yours will become mine. Luckily, I have a heart, so taking your home is pointless."

"What the fuck do you want from me?" Tracy quizzed in a low tone.

"I want you and Arrington to meet me at Longhorn in Morrow tomorrow for lunch."

Tracy rolled her eyes. If she thought she was irritated now, she would definitely want to fight me tomorrow. Fidgeting with her robe, Tracy glanced at the window and focused her attention back on me. I had this bitch exactly where I wanted her.

"Okay, but you can't tell Arrington that you came here today. Just act like it's our first time seeing each other," she instructed.

That was the shit that pissed me off about Tracy's sneaky ass. She had too many secrets, but it was only a matter of time before the shit hit the fan. She could act delirious all she wanted. I knew the truth. Since I was a little girl, I had seen past her pretty face and high yellow skin complexion. Tracy was a monster, and if she didn't tread lightly, her luxurious lifestyle was going to change drastically. I didn't need to tell Arrington; she'd find out about Tracy soon enough. I left Tracy standing there looking silly as I practically skipped down the driveway.

"Oh, and tell Dion I said hello." I laughed as I got back into my Uber.

Sighing, I leaned my head back into the seat and closed my eyes. I had stirred up enough trouble for the day. I needed to go home and get some rest. Demi didn't know how much help she'd been in such a short time. I made a mental note to send her some flowers. She deserved it.

# Chapter 4
## Arrington Parker

"How does this look? You know I'm going to see your father in the morning," my mother, Tracy, asked as she came twirling out of the dressing room.

The yellow sun dress complemented her tawny skin tone and covered her legs just enough so the guards wouldn't turn her around. Lately, she had complained about the guards turning her around before the visit started. Ten years was a long time to be incarcerated in a federal prison. The good news was that he was due to come home in less than a year. During those years, my mother never missed a phone call or a visit. They'd been married for almost twenty-three years and were the epitome of what black love should be.

In my eyes, their marriage would've been perfect had he not cheated on Mama with that nasty hoe Charae. Then, he had the nerve to get her pregnant. Even though Chauncy wasn't my biological father, he'd been with Mama since she was six months pregnant with me. He was the only dad I knew or even acknowledged. I didn't think they would've told me, either. I only found out because I asked Mama why she didn't have pictures with Daddy before her pregnancy. Instead of making up some bogus story, she told me the truth.

At nine years old, it devastated me to learn that the man I'd grown to know as my father wasn't biologically my father. It never changed how he treated me. He always assured me that he would be in my life until his last breath, and I believed him. When he first went away, I was mad at him. I felt like he'd broken his promise. How could he be in my life if he was behind bars? That seemed impossible, but I was wrong. We always spoke on the phone, and he was always there to give advice when I needed it most.

I didn't see him as often as I should've, but he never faulted me for that. He always told me he put himself there, so he expected nothing from anyone. That was some real shit. Mama didn't let that stop her, though. The love she had for my father outweighed any of his wrongdoing. That wasn't always good because he'd done things that should have never been forgiven.

Then, there was Chi. I hated that she had to stay with us every summer. Every time she stepped off that plane, she was dirty and unkempt. Daddy always sent us to the mall to buy her a summer wardrobe. Mama would make sure Chi had everything she needed. Sometimes she would go as far as dressing us alike. That used to make me hate the bitch even more. Even though she had a room at our house, I still had to share with her. Out of all the things I had to share with her, sharing my parents was the worst.

I couldn't even have my friends to myself. Chi had to come too if I was invited to a birthday party. That continued well into our teenage years until my father went to jail. Mama sent Chi back home to Chicago on the first thing smoking. That was the happiest day of my adolescent life. We only saw her again once she got kicked out of college. Even then, Mama wouldn't allow her to stay with us. I never knew why she got expelled, but it happened before Charae passed. I think Mama knew why but wasn't telling me.

"Are you sure it's not too short?" Mama asked, pulling me from my thoughts.

"It's not. Now, get dressed, so we can go eat," I urged, my eyes darting toward the dressing room. We had been shopping all day, and I was tired and hungry.

Usually, I spent my off days at home relaxing, but Mama swore she needed help finding something to wear. My boyfriend, Rylo, was busy working, so why not spend the day with her? It would make the time go by faster.

Thirty minutes later, we were at Longhorn Steakhouse for lunch. We were meeting Chi to discuss her coming to work at the shop. I didn't want her there, but Mama had the final say since it was her shop. Once we reached the table, I noticed Chi eating while nursing a mojito.

Mama sat down without speaking, and I followed suit. To this very day, I still couldn't believe Chauncy had a baby on my mother. We were always expected to treat her like royalty, which pissed me off. Every time I looked at Chi, it was a constant reminder of how her presence ruined our family.

The waiter came over and took our orders. As usual, I went with a grilled chicken strawberry salad with extra almonds and water. I always ate clean because I couldn't imagine life being over two hundred pounds like Chi.

"Well, hello, Chicago." Mama faked a smile.

"Tracy, please. You can skip the pleasantries. You don't like me, and I don't like yo' ass either. The only thing we have in common is Chauncy," she spewed, rolling her eyes in my direction."

This bitch was bold. I hadn't seen or spoken to her in years and refused to tolerate the disrespect. Chi acted like she was better than us, but we all knew that was the furthest thing from the truth. She was the bottom of the barrel, and I felt she needed a reminder of where she came from.

"Don't talk to Mama like that. Let's not forget how she took you in and accepted you, even though you were the result of Chauncy's infidelity!"

Mama had a shocked expression like she expected more out of me. "Arrington Renee Parker!"

"Nah, I'm not letting her act like she's doing us a favor. That is your shop. She can't come up here talking crazy and then think you're supposed to help her."

Mama didn't say anything because she knew I was right. She didn't have to tolerate Chi's disrespect, nor did I. At first, I felt sorry for the girl because I heard she had lost her job over a month ago. She got what she deserved.

"Girl, I will talk to her however I choose to. I'm not a little girl anymore. The days of y'all bullying me and treating me like shit are long gone, my baby. Play with me if you want to, Arrington. You gon' fuck around and find out," Chi said, rolling her neck.

I played it cool because we were in a public place, and I didn't want to embarrass Mama. If she let her work in the shop after this, she would be crazy.

The waiter returned with our food, but I no longer had an appetite. When Royce asked me if Chi could work in the shop, I should've told her ass no. Mama would've never known if it weren't for me opening my big mouth.

"Okay, that's enough. All you two ever do is fight. We're family. We must find some common ground," Mama pleaded.

"We don't have to find a thing. Here's the problem, Tracy. Both you and this air-headed hoe somehow forgot that my daddy's money started the shop in the first place. Imagine his surprise if he found out his wife and precious little step-daughter kept me from working there. That's not why I came here. I'll mop the ocean before I ever work in the shop with you, bitch." She glared in my direction. "Tracy, you know why I'm here, don't you? I want controlling interest in the shop," Chi revealed.

Mama and Chi stared each other down for what seemed like an eternity.

"Or what?"

"Or I tell my father how you two bitches treated me all those years. I remember how y'all would treat me like royalty while in front of him. The minute he left, y'all would be mean and talk badly about me. Well, I'm sure that won't be happening anymore." She laughed.

I was trying to figure out what the fuck was so funny.

"Girl, he'll never believe that shit."

"Maybe not, but I bet he will believe me when I tell him how you really get down." She smirked.

As soon as the words left her lips, Mama's face turned a bright shade of red.

"Mama, what is she talking about?"

"I don't know. Chi is fucking delusional. Get your stuff. We're leaving."

My nostrils flared as I took in each word. For years, Chi had never failed to remind me that Chauncy was her father and not mine. It was like she wanted to hurt me intentionally. Which was one of the main reasons we never got along and probably never would. I knew exactly where this conversation was going. Pushing my plate away from me, I stood up with Mama as we dismissed ourselves from the table before I had to beat Chi's ass.

Pissed was an understatement. After I made sure Mama pulled off safely, I power walked to my Lamborghini truck and pulled out my phone to call Sydney. Somebody had to hear about this shit. Chi threatened Mama, and I had to sit there and allow it. Then she wanted to mention that the money belonged to Daddy. Chi was an evil bitch who didn't deserve to have a father as good as Chauncy. She deserved to grow up poor. I needed to tell somebody about the bullshit I'd just witnessed.

Sydney and I had been cool since I first started doing hair in the shop. She had been a loyal client, and over the years, we'd become friends. The only thing I didn't like about Sydney was that she had a trifling ass baby daddy who she took care of. They shared three kids, and she was doing everything by herself while he ran the streets and spent up all her money.

"Hey, girl, are you at home? I need to vent," I said, letting out a long, exasperated sigh.

"Yeah, come on. I need an excuse to pour me a drink or two, anyway." She laughed.

Ten minutes later, I pulled up to her apartment in the projects. When I stepped out of the car, I hit my lock button twice, just in case. I had about two hours to spare before it started getting dark. Everybody knew that if you weren't from the projects, you didn't come around at night. Hell, I was taking a tremendous risk coming during the day, but Chi had me so fucked up that I had to talk about it with someone other than my mother.

Fortunately for me, I wasn't familiar with this way of living. I'd always had the best of everything for as long as I could remember. If I wasn't cool with Sydney, you wouldn't catch me stepping foot in this dump that people were forced to call home. I would've invited Sydney over to my house, but her kids were bad as hell. I had too many expensive things in my apartment for me to let her bad ass kids fuck it up.

As I approached Sydney's building, I could smell the piss reeking from the breezeway. Trash littered the sidewalks as the kids ran around, playing in the dirt. You knew it was bad when there wasn't even grass on the ground. The deplorable conditions these people were expected to live in should've been illegal.

"Damn, you fine, shawty. Can I take you out?" A man with a missing tooth approached me.

I hadn't made it to the door before he was hounding me. To make matters even worse, the missing tooth bandit smelled just like a distillery. The other two men who were sitting there just stared at me, which made me feel uncomfortable.

"No, thank you. I have a man." I smiled as I stepped around him to get to Sydney's apartment. I wanted to curse his ass out for thinking a bitch like me would ever give him the time of the day, but I knew better. These days, men couldn't take rejection and would end up killing you just because you didn't want to talk to them.

"Hey girl, you look cute," Sydney complimented as I stepped inside. "I made us some margaritas."

Sydney lived in the projects, but you couldn't tell from the inside. She always kept her house clean and smelling good. How she did it was a mystery to me because she stayed complaining about how nasty her baby daddy, Travis, was and how he never cleaned up. For the life of me, I didn't understand why she wouldn't put his ass out. It wasn't like he had anything to offer anyway.

"Girl, I am definitely in need of a drink or three," I joked as I sat on her sofa.

"So, what's going on with you?"

So much had transpired within our thirty-minute lunch that I didn't know where to begin. For starters, I found it odd that Chi had just come out of nowhere, demanding shit. Then again, Chauncy was scheduled to be released in less than a year. After I finished giving Sydney the run down, she made us another margarita.

"Damn, she's bold. What did Tracy say about it?"

"We haven't talked about it yet. I have to go over to her house in the morning. I'm sure we'll talk about it then. Anyway, enough about that bitch. You should come shopping with me tomorrow. I gotta get my man something nice for our four-year anniversary." I grinned.

Technically, we weren't official, but Sydney didn't need to know that. I was fucking the most wanted man in the city. Of course, I had to put my spin on it to keep the bitches from flocking to him.

"Y'all should be married by now."

Sydney always wanted details on my life, so I gave them to her. I didn't think she was a hater at all. I felt like she lived vicariously through me since her life was so basic. It didn't take a rocket scientist to figure out that she was miserable in her relationship.

"Oh, like you and Travis?" I shot back.

Sydney rolled her eyes as she took another sip of her margarita.

"Girl, let me get home, so I can get some rest," I said after finishing my drink.

* * *

The next morning, I woke up early and drove over to my mother's house. She still lived in the same house I grew up in. The only difference was that she had paid a construction company to fully renovate. She wanted my father to come home to their house looking better than he last remembered, and so far, she'd done a great job. When I made it there, she'd already prepared breakfast and coffee, which was a good thing because I was starving.

"She can't be serious." I laughed.

After yesterday's shenanigans, I needed a few hours to

process what the fuck had happened. Chi was serious about owning a share in our business, and I wasn't having it. There was no way I would let her take everything we'd worked so hard to build. Chauncy's money started the business, but make no mistake, our work ethic and knowledge kept the shop afloat. I recruited the best of the best, and I stood on that. If my mother gave her controlling interest, Chi would vote me out with no problem, and where would that leave me? I couldn't say I would be broke because I knew my nigga would continue to pay all my bills.

"She is, and we need to figure out what to do about it."

"What do you mean? What is she talking about?" I asked for the third time.

Whatever secret Mama harbored had to be bad because she usually told me everything. The look on her face showed concern. Like she was in fear of something. How could I help in any way if she didn't tell me what the fuck was going on?

"Just leave it alone, Arrington. If you're going to ask all these questions, I'll get this figured out on my own," she snapped.

"I'm just trying to help."

"Well, help me figure out how to get rid of her ass."

"What are you suggesting?" I quizzed, peering at my mother. Her eyes were dark. At that moment, I knew exactly what she was referring to.

I hated Chi to the core of me. Whatever she had on my mom had to be deep because getting rid of Chi was crazy. I'd done many things in my life, but 'getting rid' of a person had never been one of them. I didn't think there was anything in this world deep enough to take me there. I was all for helping Mama. However, I wasn't risking my freedom for it. There had to be another way.

Mama stood from the table and started pacing back and

forth. Something I'd never witnessed her do in my entire twenty-five years of life. Maybe I would do a little investigating of my own to try and figure out what she was hiding since she wouldn't tell me. I was sure whatever it was, it would damage her marriage. It was asinine to think it would be anything else. Had she been cheating on my father all these years? Shit, it wasn't far-fetched. I didn't know many people who could be faithful to a nigga in prison for over ten years. I didn't give a fuck what type of bag a nigga was checking. I needed dick. Unless they had conjugal visits, I was as good as gone the minute a nigga got knocked. I admired her loyalty because being married for over twenty years wasn't easy. To make matters worse, my father had been in prison for almost half that time.

"You're smart enough to draw your own conclusions," she stated without so much as batting an eyelash.

What was even more fucked up was that I was starting to believe she was serious. I'd never witnessed Mama be anything but loving. She was so caring and giving to the people around her. The woman who stood before me had become someone I didn't recognize. Furthermore, we didn't keep shit from each other. My mother was my best friend, and I trusted her with my life.

"Maybe I should go home, and we can revisit this conversation but with a different outcome. Plus, I need to be at the shop early in the morning."

Mama sighed heavily and sat down at the dining room table. The worried expression on her face was worsening. I didn't know how to help her if she refused to tell me what was wrong. I would leave it alone for now. My man hadn't called in a few days, and I was two seconds from pulling up on his ass.

"Arrington, did you hear me?" she asked, interrupting my thoughts.

"Huh?" I made sure not to hide the irritation in my voice.

"There's nothing to think about. I'm not dealing with her shit. From the day she came into my house, she's been nothing but trouble. I tried so hard to like her. I did. All that woe is me shit only made it worse," Mama complained.

Chi was very outspoken and always had something to say. She couldn't shut up if her life depended on it. From a child until now, she still had a slick ass mouth. I wish I could've gotten away with half the shit Chi did when we were younger. Since I was the oldest, I was told to set an example.

\* \* \*

"Royce, you told Chi to come work up here?" I asked, passing the flat iron through my client's hair.

Royce was usually talkative, so I knew exactly what her silence meant. She was always trying to be the peacemaker, and it was exhausting. Honestly, I didn't want the bitch working there, but obviously, she had other plans. When Chi revealed that she wanted a controlling interest in the shop, it shocked me. It was audacious, and someone needed to put her low-life ass back in her place. Chi didn't know shit about luxury until she came into our lives.

"You know we need another stylist, Arrington. That's your sister."

I waited to see if she would elaborate. I wanted to hear this bitch tell me out loud that Chi had been fired. If it were up to Royce, I would never know because she acted like everything was top secret. She never talked about her personal life or her girlfriend, Alex. If I hadn't seen her with my own two eyes, I would almost think she didn't exist. I tried to be as cool as I could with Royce since Alex was Rylo's sister. I felt like if I hung around her, I would see Rylo more often since she claimed to see him more than I did. That was one thing that pissed me off to no end. How did the next bitch get to see my man several times a week? Well, Rylo and I hadn't made things official. We did everything as a couple, and I was content with that. I knew our situation wasn't ideal, but he was a paid nigga.

"We good. If we needed another stylist, I'd hire one," I snapped, discreetly rolling my eyes.

Royce continued cutting her client's hair without saying another word. She knew better than to challenge me. I was part owner of this shop and would kick her ass out if it came down to it. I wanted to tell her how much of a disrespectful bitch Chi was, but I knew Royce would be ready to fight about her precious little cousin. I didn't need that type of drama popping off.

"Are y'all talking about the girl who does wig installs?" my client, Carla, asked. Royce nodded her head. "She's the best in the city. I was sad when she closed her books." She nervously laughed.

Damn, that stung. In so many words, she said that I was her second option. I started to slap her in the back of her black ass neck since she thought the shit was funny. It was all good, however. Since she liked Chi so much, I would block her from my books. There wasn't a bitch I knew bold enough to tell me that Chi was their first option. Carla had shit twisted. If I weren't professional, I would have kicked her out of my chair, bald cap and all. She had better enjoy it. This would be the last time I installed her synthetic ass wig.

Later that evening, I sat on my couch, scrolling through social media, when I received a text from my man Rylo. He told me to be ready in thirty minutes and that he sent me a car. My coochie started jumping, thinking about how good Rylo would dick me down. We hadn't seen each other in days, so I knew he missed me.

I loved Rylo, but he was distant. We had been dealing with each other for the past four years, and I honestly didn't see myself with anybody else. He provided financial security and could fuck me good. What else did I need? I was the type of bitch you wouldn't catch dead with a broke nigga. I knew he dealt with other bitches occasionally, but that went with the territory. Long as he kept my pockets laced, that was all that mattered.

Quicker than lightning speed, I jumped in the shower, oiled my body down with my lavender-infused body oil, and placed my long weave in a low ponytail. I threw on my Skims body shaper as an outfit with a kimono and a pair of Gucci slides. I dabbed behind my ears with my favorite Christian Dior scent and applied a fresh coat of lip gloss. After completing a once-over in my full-length mirror, I grabbed my hoe bag and was out the door.

Rylo was the type of nigga you had to be prepared for. The nigga was impatient and didn't like to wait long. In all the years we'd dealt with each other, he had never been inside my apartment. What hurt most about our relationship was that it was hard to get Rylo to open up. I barely knew anything about his personal life. The only person who knew anything about him was his right hand, Alex.

Stepping outside, I took in the cool, crisp air. The driver greeted me as he opened the door and helped me into the truck. A bottle of Belaire was on ice in the back with a wine glass. I loved dealing with a rich nigga. There were plenty of bitches who wanted to be in my position, but I wasn't coming up off Rylo. He was that nigga.

It took over an hour to make it to Rylo's estate. By then, I was three glasses in and tipsy. The driver pulled into the gate as I hurriedly pulled my compact mirror out of my purse to check my appearance. My skin was flushed from the champagne, and

I needed a fresh coat of lip gloss. Nonetheless, I was still the shit. I loved reminding myself that out of all the bitches in Atlanta, I was the chosen one.

The driver opened the door and helped me out of the truck. Rylo's butler, Rogelio, came outside, grabbed my overnight bag, and escorted me in. The aroma of food permeated my nostrils as he guided me to Rylo. The walk to the house's west wing took so long that I thought I would need an electric scooter to get me there faster. Usually, whenever I came over, we were on the east wing. This side of the house was beautiful. The design and décor were consistent with the east wing, and I loved it. I often imagined moving in and showing off the house to my friends. Even though I didn't reside there, I was still ahead of any other bitch I knew. Especially Chi's broke down ass. She could never be on my level.

"Mr. Lopez, your evening guest has arrived," he announced as if I were his second guest of the day.

We entered what appeared to be a theater room. The room had a projector and luxurious recliner chairs across five rows. There was also a concession stand with a popcorn maker and a soda fountain machine. Rylo stared at me intently with lust-filled eyes.

"Hey, baby," I cooed.

Rylo nodded like I was one of his homeboys instead of his girlfriend. I hated when he did that shit. His eyes said one thing, but his body language said otherwise. The proper way to greet me was with a kiss. Hell, he was the one who sent for me. He could've acted like he was happy to see a bitch.

"Sup, you hungry?" he quizzed, walking right past me.

"No. I thought we were going to watch a movie together. You had Rogelio bring me to the theater room that I never knew existed. What else is on this side of the house?" I questioned as I followed Rylo.

He was a very private man. At times, that shit pissed me off. I'd known this man for four years and hadn't even met his mother. When I would ask about it, he always told me he had never introduced any woman to his mother because she was too critical. I didn't believe that bullshit.

Once we made it to the dining room, I took in the aroma of seafood. The chef had prepared blackened salmon with shrimp, mashed potatoes, and asparagus. A call came through, and Rylo excused himself from the table and instructed me to start eating without him. He never discussed business in front of me or anyone else. Many different stories circulated regarding his line of work. So many that I didn't know which to believe. From my observations, he seemed to be into some of everything. It was one of those, the less I knew, the better situations. It didn't bother me because I knew his real name. I would've never known if it had not been for a piece of mail I spotted lying on his kitchen counter. Even though I knew, it took him months to tell me his birth-given name.

People said he sold drugs and was the largest distributor on the southeast coast. Some believed he was a cold-blooded killer. However, I doubted a man dressed in a suit and tie was knocking mothafuckas off every day. I'd know if I was fucking a killer. He did socialize with politicians often. Rylo knew the mayor personally and had his number on speed dial. That alone spoke volumes as to the type of man he was.

"I didn't keep you waiting too long, did I?" Rylo asked, walking back into the dining room.

The truth was, I was pissed. I'd eaten my entire meal and finished half a glass of wine. Why the fuck did he call me over there if he wasn't going to eat dinner with me or pay me any attention? It was after ten at night. He had all day to talk business on the phone, and I was ready for some dick. I understood he was busy, but I needed his attention too. After taking another sip of wine, I took the napkin out of my lap and wiped the corners of my mouth.

"No, baby, but I miss you," I pouted. The wine in my system had me ready to knock all this shit over and ride him on this expensive ass table. His smooth, calm demeanor turned me on.

"Show me." He smirked, sitting on the dining room chair.

Licking my lips, I got on my knees and unbuckled his pants.

# Chapter 5
## *Rylo*

I woke up beside a sleeping Arrington. Usually, I didn't let her spend the night, but she sucked my dick so good it put a nigga to sleep. Had me feeling like a lil bitch the way I was clutching the back of her head. I mainly called her when I needed some pussy or someone to accompany me to one of the mayor's events. Lately, she was the only female I could stand being around. I was selective about who I stuck dick to. Fucking any female with a hole wasn't my style. Most of them were either star-struck or tried to demand shit from a nigga. Not Arrington. She knew how to play her position.

I met Arrington during one of the worst times of my life, and she was there for a nigga, so in return, I held her down financially. It was the least I could do because I refused to let a bitch have full access to me. Initially, I explained to her that dealing with me would have stipulations. I told her to let me know if she couldn't handle it. Ultimately, she agreed, and we'd been fucking around ever since.

Having her around was cool until she started asking too many questions.

I chose to keep my life private for a reason. Arrington

talked too fucking much, and I didn't want to end up having to smoke her ass for telling my business to the wrong person. That's how niggas ended up getting caught up or killed. I wasn't trying to die any time soon, so I moved accordingly.

I was stacking up all this money with nobody to leave it to besides my mother. My sister, Alex, was straight. Getting money came easy to her because she had me as a mentor. After our brother Brandon died, she took it upon herself to learn the business.

Alex was my right hand and the only person I trusted. There was no need for her to prove her loyalty to me. We were bonded by blood, and our mother raised us on loyalty. Our father left after she was born, so the older I got, the more protective I became. The best part was that I didn't have to worry about knocking a nigga's lungs back because Alex was a lesbian. Shit, I noticed that by the time she was five years old. Our mother swore up and down that her only girl would be just like her. When Alex finally came out, she supported her and treated her no differently. Alex was unaware that our mother cried every night for months, and I'd never tell her.

"Hmm, hey you." Arrington yawned, garnering my attention. "You should stay in bed with me." She smiled.

Arrington had gotten lucky by me allowing her to spend the night, but her time was up. Today was Monday, and I had business to handle. Shit wasn't going to get done lying around in bed all day. I hadn't obtained this level of success by bullshitting around. I was up by 6:00 a.m. daily and out the door for my morning jog by 7:00.

That was another reason I didn't want to be exclusive. I couldn't commit my time to anything other than the money. It called me day and night. I never hesitated to answer. It reminded me of how I took the streets by force years ago. A nigga was still running shit, but it was on some behind-the-scenes shit. Alex oversaw the day-to-day operations of my former distribution business. It was easy because she didn't have to deal with the corner boys who sold dime bags. She was now the plug. I only had to step in for her when negotiating with the Columbian Cartel. They weren't particularly fond of doing business with women.

I had no doubts that she could hold her own. The problem was that men lacked respect for women in this line of business. I always had a watchful eye on Alex. I couldn't have niggas thinking shit was sweet. I'd kill a nigga's whole family if I had to. I would be a lying mothafucka to act like that was above me. I was a suit and tie-wearing nigga, but I was with all the fuck shit.

"Can we at least sleep in until nine? I think I had too many glasses of wine," Arrington mumbled. "Also, I wanted to talk to you about our situation, Rylo. We've been dealing with each other for a while. Is this all we're ever going to do? I mean, we are past the point of putting a title on things. We've both been in each other's corner, which speaks volumes as to how we feel about each other. I guess what I'm trying to say is, I think we should make things official. We do everything just like a normal couple. I don't see why not." She shrugged.

My jaw tightened. Arrington and I being in a relationship had never crossed my mind. This wasn't the first time she'd brought the conversation to light. My response was always the same each time. If I wanted to be with her, then I would. Arrington wasn't relationship material. She was clingy, and I didn't want to feel suffocated. The distance I put between us was intentional.

"The car will be ready in ten minutes." That was my curt response.

I guess she thought that fake pouting shit would work on

me. If she asked again, I wouldn't be nice a second time. I wasn't there to cater to how she felt.

Ignoring her antics, I hopped out of bed and headed to the bathroom to brush my teeth. I changed into a white tee with some Nike shorts. By the time I made it back to the bedroom, Arrington had gotten dressed and ready for the driver. I made a mental note to never let that shit happen again. Whenever she came over, I always sent her ass home before I went to sleep. I'd slipped up now and would likely go a few days without hitting her up. She had an attitude, but I ain't give a fuck. Maybe next time, she would learn to keep her mouth closed. I'd hate to think she forgot about our agreement.

After finishing my morning jog, I showered and ate a light breakfast. A nigga was from the trenches, but I cared about what I put in my body. I had to stay away from Mama's crib because she was always cooking up some soul food. At 6'3", I had an athletic build with defined muscles. Eating all that unhealthy shit tasted good, but it did more harm than good in the long run. My phone buzzed on the counter.

"Sup, lil sis'?"

"Shit, about to touch base with Ronnie," she replied.

Ronnie was one of her workers who met with potential buyers to vet them before negotiating a contract. He was thorough in his work and had been successful as the middleman. It was rare that Alex had to meet with anyone. She'd done it once, but that shit made me uncomfortable. He tried to lowball my sister. When I found out about it, I killed him. I made an example out of him for any nigga who wanted to try her. So far, everything had been running smoothly, but I could never be too sure. Recruiting Ronnie proved to be beneficial. At first, Alex gave me pushback, which resulted in our first big argument. Shortly after, she reconsidered.

"Aight. I need you and Ronnie to meet me at Capital Grille for lunch."

Alex knew what type of time I was on. I was all about bringing in more money. Too much was never enough for a nigga like me. Billionaire status was the goal. I was twenty-two when I made my first million, but now that shit was like chump change. My mind was always brainstorming some shit, but I was sure I hit the jackpot with this one. More money equaled more problems, but I was willing to take that risk. I was built for this shit.

"Everything good?"

I heard the concern in her voice. She knew I still struggled with the death of Brandon. I relived that shit every single day I opened my eyes. That shit had fucked with me mentally. Alex suggested seeing a therapist, but I was a street nigga turned made nigga. I ain't believe in shit like that. There was no way I was paying a mothafucka to tell me how they think I should handle my problems. I was the only person who could control that.

Even though it had been five years since Brandon's passing, it still consumed my mind every waking second of the day. Going to sleep didn't make it better, either. My dreams of him were vivid, as if he were still with us. My brother would never return. Accepting that was the hardest part.

\* \* \*

I walked into Capital Grille at eleven forty-five sharp. The way I saw it, if you were on time, you were late. Timing was everything. Being disciplined was only hard if you made it that way. I waited another ten minutes before the waitress showed me to my table. As expected, Alex and Ronnie were there waiting for me. When Alex started in this business, I taught her how important time was. Everybody had the same twenty-four hours, so there were no excuses for not getting to the money. Sometimes, I had to remember that Alex had a girl. She was adamant about making sure she spent enough time with her.

"Sup, my boy? You look dapper than a muthafucka, twin," she complimented as she stood to hug me.

I was always happy to see my sister. She reminded me of our mother. Instead, she dressed like a nigga. I had to give it to her. She was fresh in her button-down and black slacks. After Ronnie dapped me up, I sat down, and we got straight to business. I glanced over my shoulder to ensure no familiar faces were in the room. These days, it was easy to follow somebody and study their day-to-day habits. I knew because I'd done it more times than I could count. The best time to drop a mothafucka was when he least expected it and was comfortable in his surroundings. There were plenty of niggas who wanted me dead, but my movements were always calculated. I was no fool, so I kept a security detail around the clock. I couldn't be caught lacking like the rest of these goofy ass niggas.

"Check your phones. I just airdropped a file," I instructed.

Both Alex and Ronnie checked their phones and began to go over the document. The nigga trying to do business with me was the mayor's nephew. Sterling White. He had been into politics since college, but something about him wanting to do business with me was alarming. He had money, power, and respect in Atlanta. He would never have the same respect from the streets because he wasn't from the trenches. There had to be a bigger picture I couldn't see. That was where Ronnie came in.

As we reviewed his file, I gave Ronnie specific instructions on what I needed him to find out. I wanted him to go back to his high school years if he could. I needed all the information I could find before setting up a meeting. It was tricky working with niggas in politics because they were known to be some grimy mothafuckas. Grim Reaper was my middle name, and I had no problem blowing a nigga's top.

"The mayor's nephew?" Alex whispered. "I don't know about this, Rylo. You might have to pass on this one," she advised.

"No, I think there are some potential money avenues here," Ronnie countered.

Alex shook her head as she continued to read over the file.

"He has connections. The fuck does he need us for?" Alex questioned.

That was the one question that lingered. Part of me wanted to see how far this shit could go because it would bring in an additional five million dollars. I was all about new business endeavors but at what cost? There had to be something that we didn't know about Sterling.

"Is he looking for investors?"

Alex was picking up fast, which was a good thing. Over the last few years, I'd invested more than a million dollars in small companies in the Atlanta area. I owned a share in over twenty-five companies, which proved very lucrative. Sterling wanted me to invest in his new business venture, which sounded good, but I knew how shit worked with his kind. I could bet all my money that this business proposal was a front.

"Hello, my name is Cassie, and I'll be your server today. Can I start you all with any drinks or appetizers?" After she took our orders, we continued to discuss Sterling's file.

"He is looking for investors. First, we gon' let Ronnie do his thing before we make any decisions. Let's not forget that he has a reputation to uphold. I'm sure this is something Mayor White is aware of."

Over the years, I'd worked hard to clean up my image. I didn't need help fucking that up. If Sterling was on some other shit, he was a dead man. I didn't give a fuck about him being related to the mayor. Ronnie guaranteed he would do his part as the waiter brought our food. Once we were finished, I paid for our meal and left the waitress a nice tip just because she was fine. Alex rode with Ronnie. He lived north of Buckhead, so driving her to Jonesboro would take him out of his way. I told him that I would take her home. Plus, I had to stop at my rental property out in McDonough.

Alex was quiet on the ride to her house. I could tell she wasn't feeling the Sterling situation. I had a feeling it was more to the story. Alex never gave pushback about any of my clients. She always trusted my decisions but had been tense since I mentioned his name.

"You want to tell me what's going on?"

"It ain't my story to tell, bruh. I just know he did some fucked up shit a few years ago, back when he was in college, and I can't vibe with that shit. I'm telling you, Rylo, that nigga is bad for business. I know you want that deal, but just listen to me this one time." She pleaded—something I'd never witnessed.

"First, how you know the nigga? He did something to you? I'll go kill that nigga right now."

"Nah, he ain't did shit to me. Can you just do me a solid and trust my word?"

That was the difference between us. Rightfully so, she made decisions solely based on emotions. As for me, that would be detrimental to my money. Every move I made had to be logical. Shit had to be analyzed from every angle. I'd done business with some ruthless mothafuckas in the past. Niggas knew better than to try me. My name rang bells for a reason. Whatever business endeavor I went into, I always weighed out the shit that could potentially go wrong. I hated disappointing

Alex, but I stood firm on my decision. Sometimes in this business, you have to take risks.

"Aye, man, wasup with Arrington? She keeps trying to come to the crib and hang with Royce, knowing she doesn't fuck with her like that. Royce said she keeps asking questions about you and shit." Alex laughed.

Our situation was nothing more than us fucking, but Arrington was ready for something more. I understood. However, I just couldn't give her that. Royce had probably told her how often I visited their house. She hoped to catch me there one day to convince me to let her come to the crib. Arrington was starting to get too attached. It was time to start distancing myself. I wasn't with all that clingy shit.

"She trippin'. I'ma talk to her about it." I made a mental note to check Arrington. I didn't like the fact that she was running around asking questions.

"I don't like that bitch anyway. Something about her is off. I feel like she is the type to start moving funny if you do something she doesn't like. She's been tripping on Royce about her sister."

"Arrington has a sister?" I'd known her for four years. She never mentioned having a sister.

"Damn, that's weird. Royce is with her all the time. I'm surprised you never met her. Then again, her nigga is always tripping about her hanging out with Royce so much.

"Well, if she didn't tell me, she must not want me to know." I wasn't pressed to find out what Arrington had going on in her life. It wasn't my business if it wasn't interfering with me or my money.

"She can't stand her. Royce made that clear. I just want to know why she keeps asking about Brandon."

I didn't have an answer, but I would find out. Arrington knew that Brandon was off limits. Talking about him only made me sink deeper into the dark hole I'd been fighting to escape. Honestly, there was nothing to know about him other than he had more motion than any nigga in the city. Brandon's death would forever take a toll on me. It took a toll on the whole hood. Shit, mothafuckas came from across the country to his services to pay their respect. That was real shit.

The thing about losing a loved one was that everybody continued with their lives after the casket dropped. I couldn't move on just yet. I don't know if I ever would. I'd never forget the last image I had of him. I would have to live with that for the rest of my life, which fucked me up. Losing a sibling was a different type of hurt. It broke my mother's heart to lose a child. I didn't know how to help her through that shit. I knew Brandon would want me to make sure she was straight.

After I dropped Alex off, I checked on my rental property for a final walk-through before the new tenants moved in. Renting out properties wasn't something I usually did, but I was starting my own property management company. I'd been buying houses left and right. Initially, I purchased the home for Mama. She refused to move in it, claiming it was too big for her. She was nearing retirement age, and I wanted to make sure she had everything her heart desired. That included a new house. She had done the work of raising us and made sure we never went without. There were nights she went without eating, but it didn't matter. As long as the three of us were fed, she was satisfied.

Once my walkthrough was complete, I texted my new assistant, Mary, to let her know it was ready to be placed on the website to rent. The houses in Atlanta went fast, and I was sure there would be new tenants moving in within a few weeks.

Forty minutes later, I was riding through the hood. The engine on my Camaro roared as I bent the corners of the streets that took part in raising me. Even though I didn't come around much, I was still respected, like I ran shit. Whenever I didn't have my security detail with me, I kept my gun in my lap. I was a businessman but a street nigga before all else.

The only reason I came this way was to visit my grandfather, who was bedridden. Pops had cancer but was a true fighter. They'd given him less than a year to live, and instead of putting him in a nursing home, we chose to hire a hospice nurse to care for him. My mother went to visit him every day and always kept me updated on his condition. I pulled up in the driveway and killed the engine. When I hopped out of the car, a few people standing on the corner nodded in my direction. It was crazy how some of the niggas I grew up with were still in the hood on the same shit, fucking the same bitches. Using my key, I opened the front door and was greeted by his hospice nurse.

"Hey, Mr. Lopez." She smiled coyly.

"Sup' Shayla."

"I just gave Mr. Rickey his meds. You know how he gets when he doesn't get it on time. I was five minutes late, and he started fussing." Pops didn't play about his pain medicine.

Shayla was fine as fuck, but I didn't mix business with pleasure. I knew she wanted to fuck by the way she looked at me. She was flirtatious and touched me every chance she had. Shayla was the type of woman who knew how to use her looks to get what she wanted. I could never fuck with a female like her, though. Like Pops would say, she was a man-eater, and I ain't want no parts. Shit, I wouldn't be surprised if she fucked half the niggas on base when she was in the military. She'd been vetted by Ronnie, and I was confident she wasn't an imminent threat. Having recently moved from Italy, she had started her own home health care business and came highly recommended. So far, she had been exceptional, and I didn't want to fuck that up by giving her the dick.

"Wasup, Pops," I greeted as I sat in the recliner next to his bed.

"Hey, grandson. You bring me something to snack on?"

He was so enthralled by Family Feud that he didn't even look in my direction. According to Mama, Pops had been watching the show since it first aired in the seventies. It had easily become his favorite show. I tried to visit as often as I could, but between Mama and Shayla, I knew he was in good hands. Shayla made sure he had everything he needed. I even paid her extra to do his grocery shopping. For months, I'd been trying to convince Mama to let me hire a cleaning service, but she wasn't having it. She would tell me nobody knew how Pops liked his house but her, and she stood on that. Every time I came over, the house was clean and smelled good.

"Come on now, Pops, you know I never come empty-handed."

"You better not unless you want me to get out the bed and kick yo' ass," he joked. "Where's your big-headed sister?"

"At home. I just dropped her off a few hours ago." Silence filled the room. Pops had something to say; I knew him like the back of my hand.

"You know, eventually, you need to let her run that business how she sees fit," he advised.

Pops ran the streets back in the day, but the minute my grandmother got pregnant, and Mama was born, he changed his life. He knew what I did and always gave me advice from his past experiences.

"I'm just trying to protect her. Messing with the Columbians is risky. She needs to be groomed, Pops. It's not something you can just walk into."

Pops shook his head and turned the TV off. That was when I knew shit was about to get serious. He never turned Family Feud off for anybody, not even Mama. At eighty-five years old, he was full of knowledge and wisdom, and I soaked it all in. I could only hope to live as long as he did. Although he had cancer, he didn't let that bring him down.

"Listen to me, son. Before I leave this earth, I need you to understand something. Tomorrow ain't promised. You gotta let go of that guilt you been holding onto since Brandon passed. It wasn't your fault, and there's nothing you can do to bring him back. Ya' hear me? Don't forget, you let her assume the position. I know you're trying to protect her, but Alex is smart. She knows what she's doing. Don't make the mistake of hovering over her. Allow her to become who she needs to be for the business to thrive, son. She's capable of making the right decisions, and you know it just as well as I do.

Pops had a point. I was steadily holding on to the guilt of losing Brandon. It wasn't like I wanted to; it just wouldn't go away. Had I made it there a second sooner, he would still be alive today. I'd introduced him to this life and wasn't there when he needed me the most. I was supposed to be the one lying six feet under, not him.

"Well, let me get up out of here, old man. I got a few more corners to bend before I head in for the night."

Pops shook his head and turned the TV back on. "That's your problem now, Ryan. Can't nobody get through to yo' ass. Keep holding onto that guilt. It's going to destroy you, son," he warned. "That's not what Brandon would want for you."

That was one of the many reasons I kept my distance from family. Everybody always tried to tell me how I should feel when they weren't the ones who found my brother's lifeless body lying in the middle of an alley. Without another word, I stood up and left. I didn't even bother to tell him I would see him later. He'd pissed me off. Instead of saying something I'd regret, I chose to make an exit.

"See you later, Mr. Lopez," Shayla said as I walked past her.

I wish shit was as easy as people made it seem. Grief didn't have an expiration date. I had the right to feel how I wanted to feel. His death was my fault, and I didn't deserve to be breathing, so I made money my priority to mask my true feelings. I didn't deserve to be happy or in a thriving relationship. I wasn't worthy of love because all I would do was hurt whatever woman came into my life. Arrington included.

When I made it outside to my car, I noticed my tire was a little low. I couldn't put on the spare because I still hadn't put it back in the trunk from the last time I used it. There was no point in having a spare if I was going to leave it sitting in my garage. I pulled out my phone to call my car service but was interrupted by Shayla coming outside behind me.

"Everything okay?"

"Yeah. My tire going flat, and my spare is at home in the garage."

"I know someone who has a shop right up the street."

After she gave me the directions to the shop, I wasted no time going to get a replacement tire. It would have to do until I could get another one from Michelin. The guy who ran the shop introduced himself as Baron. He was fast and efficient, which was more than I could say for most black-owned tire shops. I made sure to tip him a couple hundred because I respected a nigga who made his money legitimately. Before I left, I told Baron I would refer people to him if they were in the area.

# Chapter 6
## *Royce*

"**W**hy the fuck do you keep playing with me, Royce? Damn."

Alex was sitting on the toilet, taking a shit, when I played a prank on her. It all started when she asked me to bring her a toilet paper roll out of the linen closet. Alex always forgot to put toilet paper in the bathroom. She didn't know I'd purchased a fake roll of tissue that didn't tear from Amazon.

"What? I didn't even do anything." I chuckled.

"You a lie. If you are innocent, then why is this toilet paper so strong? They don't sell shit like this at the store. Quit playing and bring a roll of toilet paper, Royce," Alex yelled on the other side of the door.

I tiptoed to the front door and grabbed my keys off the entryway table to run an errand. She would have to get it herself, shitty booty and all. I wanted to teach her ass a lesson. There was nothing I hated more than going to use the restroom, and there wasn't any tissue. What was so hard about replacing the roll?

Instead of going back home, I pulled up on Chi since she

still didn't have her car. Of course, Baron didn't like it, but I didn't give a fuck. Hanging out with my cousin was more important than anything. We'd been close since the day I met her. We were opposite of each other. I think that was why we got along so great. Baron thought Chi was supposed to spend all her time with him. He barely wanted her to work. When we were younger, my uncle Chauncy always told us it was essential to make your own money. Now, I see why he instilled that in us.

Growing up, I used to say I wanted to be like his wife, Tracy. She was beautiful, had the perfect body, and what I thought was the ideal life. She didn't have to work a job because my uncle was the provider. It wasn't until I was older that I realized men used that as a control tactic. I learned that the hard way from my previous relationship. Being a kept bitch was all good until you had to deal with a plethora of bitches claiming to have fucked your man. Or women popping out with babies, which was a deal breaker. At least for me, it was.

My last boyfriend, Tommy, had taken me through hell and back, and it took a long time for me to heal from that toxic ass nigga. Getting hurt by someone you loved was the worst pain, and I didn't wish it on anyone.

To make a long story short, some female he had been dealing with came to the shop talking about she was pregnant with his baby and that he was her man. Instead of trying to fight her, I told her she could have his low-life ass. I no longer wanted him. He'd crossed that line and had to stay there.

Then, Alex came along and mended a heart she didn't break. She showed me a love I thought I would never be worthy of. Before I met her, I wasn't into girls. I always thought women were beautiful, but not in a romantic way. Alex was gentle and caring and showed me daily that she worshipped the ground I walked on. She still showed me genuine love, even when I had my days and lashed out at her.

I pulled up to Chi's apartment in less than fifteen minutes. Sometimes I missed when we used to live together. Our late-night talks got me through tough times, but I never told her that. When I walked through the door, I could tell she had just fried some chicken. Hopefully, she had some more because a bitch was hungry. I couldn't cook to save my life, so eating at Chi's saved me some coins. If Alex didn't cook, we'd probably starve to death fucking around with me.

"It smells good in here, cousin. I want some."

"I bet yo' beggin' ass do," Byron joked as I sat on the sofa.

Byron and I had a love-hate type of relationship. Simply put, he wanted me but couldn't have me. He always made slick comments, but I ignored his ass every single time. Byron needed to realize that even if I was single, his ass was too young for me. He was still a kid. Also, Byron was in the streets more than Baron knew. He ran drugs for this nigga named Romeo, who was from around the way. Me being the loyal cousin I am, I mentioned it to Chi, but she chose to keep it to herself since she knew that Baron wouldn't believe her.

"Boy, shut up before I give you the ass whooping ya' mama should've."

"Come here. I might like it." He winked.

"Ew, Chi, come and get your brother-in-law," I screamed, running into the kitchen.

"Y'all always arguing. It makes me think y'all lowkey like each other," Chi joked.

"Bitch, don't get stomped out in your own kitchen. You know how I feel about Alex with her funky ass."

"Speaking of, she called and told me what you did. Keep playing so much, she gon' fuck around and leave your ass."

Alex knew how I was when she met me, so I highly

doubted that. She talked shit all day but didn't love me or my prankster ways any less. I was a YouTuber. What did she expect? My channel was mainly hair content, but I had to switch it up occasionally.

"Well, that's on her. She's the one always forgetting to replace the roll. Goofy ass."

Chi placed macaroni, cabbage, and fried chicken on a plate and shoved it in my direction. I grabbed a Hawaiian roll and headed back to the living room. By that time, Byron had gone into his room. I was relieved because as much as I played around, I didn't have the energy for his smart-ass mouth. If Alex knew how much he flirted with me, she'd be pissed. I didn't plan on volunteering that information now or ever.

"Any word on your car yet?

Chi sighed heavily as she plopped down on the sofa. She looked exhausted, and I had a feeling she and Baron had been arguing. Baron was like an energy vampire. He would suck all the life out of you until nothing was left. If it was exhausting for me, I could only imagine how Chi felt. Just the thought of having to deal with his bullshit made me cringe. If he were easy to get along with, I wouldn't mind being around him, but that shit was a wrap.

"I don't know. I'm just frustrated with everything. Where do I start? I don't have a job. My car is still down. I keep having to argue with this nigga. The list goes on."

"I know you don't like to feel like you're dumping your problems on me, but I'm here if you need to talk, cousin."

"Girl, I'll be okay. I be ready to knock Baron's ass upside the head sometimes," she replied, and we laughed in unison.

Chi had always been private about her life, even with me. Sometimes getting her to talk was like pulling teeth. When we were younger, she never expressed how she felt unless pushed to the edge. Undoubtedly, Arrington was good at drawing those emotions out of her.

"I won't force you with yo' stubborn ass. Anyway, I forgot how Arrington tried to check me about you the other day. She knew better than to get out of pocket with me. I don't know why that girl has so much animosity toward you."

At that point, I was getting tired of being the peacemaker. I was seeing that no matter what I did, this shit would never be resolved. Both were out for blood. Little did they know, I was throwing in the towel. I couldn't fix it, and after all these years, I was tired.

"Fuck her. She better be lucky I didn't drag her ass when we met up for lunch. I'm sick of her and her mammy," Chi fumed. "I don't know why you keep trying to get me to come work in that shithole anyway. If I didn't want to risk my freedom, I would burn that bitch down."

I knew Chi well enough to see that the situation was more profound than she let on. However, I would leave it alone until she told me. After I finished my food, I went to Chi's liquor cabinet and poured myself a shot of Don Julio. I almost poured one for Chi but remembered she was pregnant. Maybe Chi didn't want to discuss her problems, but I wanted to discuss mine.

"I think Alex is cheating on me," I revealed. Bewilderment filled Chi's almond-shaped eyes. "I mean, I'm not a hundred percent sure."

Chi jumped up, grabbed the entire bottle of liquor out of the cabinet, and shoved it in my hands. Through whatever, my girl was going to be there for me. She handed me a tulip-shaped glass half filled with margarita mix.

"Hold on. Alex adores you, Royce. Why on earth would you think she's cheating on you? You two are perfect for each other."

There was no doubt in my mind that Alex loved me, but our relationship wasn't perfect. My last relationship broke me, and I didn't want a repeat of that. I was at a place where I needed reassurance. As crazy as it sounded, I didn't want to approach Alex unless I had solid proof.

"She steps outside to answer her phone. She always says it's just business when I ask her about it. Then I overheard her on the phone making plans to go to Texas last week. I've been waiting for her to say something or at least invite me for days."

"So, invite yourself," she suggested.

What if Alex had been on the phone with another female and planned to meet her out of town? I decided to take Chi's advice. I planned to crash the party if she intended to meet someone there.

"You're right. If Alex doesn't say anything, I will pack my bags and be at the hotel right along with her. You should come with me. I think she's supposed to stay for a week."

"Royce, that sounds wild. You want me to help you stalk your girlfriend?"

"You're the one who suggested it. It wouldn't be stalking if Alex knew I was coming. Now that I think about it, I ain't telling her shit. I'm a just pop up on that ass."

Now, the liquor was talking. Alex would probably think I was a crazy bitch, but I had to see for myself. I didn't know how I would react, but I would cross that bridge once I got to it. After several more drinks and a little more convincing, Chi decided to book a flight to Houston with me the following week.

"Bitch, you better be lucky I love you. Inviting and stalking are two different things. I get that you're trying to catch her in a lie, but maybe you should ask her about the phone situation. She might have a logical reason behind it."

Now this hoe was sugarcoating shit, trying to make me feel

better. I wouldn't feel better until I got to the bottom of this. I couldn't chance Alex lying to me. If shit hit the fan, I was leaving her ass where she stood. I'd been skeptical of letting her in the way I did, fearing she would do me the same way Tommy did. The only difference was that she couldn't get another bitch pregnant.

"Ask her for what? I'm not giving her the opportunity to lie to my face. That'll crush me."

Chi and I went back and forth on how to approach the situation. Ultimately, it was my decision. I wanted to go to Houston and see what the fuck Alex was up to, and I had the perfect way of going about it.

* * *

"Will that be all for you, ma'am?" the cashier asked, placing my Apple air tag and new phone case in a bag.

It was the day before the trip, and Alex still had said nothing, but I played it cool. When I returned home, I put the air tag in her suitcase to track her location. I waited until she was gone to pack my suitcase. I didn't want her to get suspicious.

"What you doing, bae? Cleaning out the closet?" Alex questioned, walking into our bedroom.

My heart felt like it was beating a thousand miles per minute as her footsteps got closer. My hands shook as I quickly placed her suitcase back on her side of the closet. Turning off the light, I exited the closet before she could reach me.

"Oh, I was looking for a pair of shoes Chi asked me to borrow, but I didn't see them," I lied.

"What do they look like? I can help you."

Was she fucking serious? Of all things, I couldn't believe she was offering to help me look for a pair of shoes that didn't exist. Unfortunately, I was a terrible liar. Alex was the type who could smell bullshit from a mile away.

"Oh, you know what, babe? I think they're in my trunk. Let me go outside and look."

Alex tried to look for me, but I convinced her I needed to go myself. As soon as I reached my car, I dialed Chi's number.

"Hello?" she answered on the first ring. The irritation in her voice was clear.

"Did I catch you at a bad time?"

"Girl, this nigga over here tripping. I'll call you right back."

When I returned inside, Alex was on a phone call but paused once she noticed I was standing there. She looked at me as if she'd seen a ghost. She was hiding something from me. I tried to hide the disappointment on my face, but that seemed almost impossible.

"Rylo, let me call you back," she said and ended her call. "You didn't find the shoes?"

That lying shit wasn't for me. Maybe I should've listened to Chi and asked her about the trip. I'd already purchased my plane ticket and paid for the hotel. It was too late to back out now.

# Chapter 7
## *Chi*

"How you gon' book a flight to Houston and not say shit about it to me?" Baron questioned as he paced back and forth across the living room floor. "An entire week at that!"

Once again, I had cleaned up the entire house and cooked dinner, and this nigga wanted to come in the house tripping. I had planned to tell him about the impromptu trip, but apparently, Byron made it to him before I did. I couldn't believe that little fucker snitched on me when he was hiding shit from Baron.

"Nigga, why the fuck do you keep acting like you're my daddy or something? I don't need your permission to go to Houston. Lately, you have been on a power trip. I'm not feeling that."

Baron glared in my direction. He didn't like the fact that I'd exposed him. "Man, you tripping. I'm just trying to take care of you," he countered, dismissing me with a hand wave.

"Baron, you think I don't notice how you've been acting lately? You keep saying you want to keep me put up, but I didn't ask you for that. Since I got fired from my job, you never once asked me how I felt. Instead, you started deciding for me."

I had been cooking and cleaning like this perfect little housewife for over a month. Things had been rocky, and I just wanted things to go back to normal between us. I couldn't bear another month of waiting for Baron to deposit money into my account on his terms. He would lash out whenever I tried to talk to him about it. At this point, his need to control me would end up pushing me away. I loved Baron and wanted things to work, but I was conflicted.

My father always told me to never depend on a nigga. That stuck with me because Charae relied on her pussy and men to get what she wanted. Now, there I was, constrained with no plan.

Baron pulled me in for a hug. "You're right. I'm sorry, baby. I should've never assumed you wanted to be cooped up in this apartment. I grew up with my father caring for his household, and I thought that would be ideal for us. Baby, I know what you have been through in the past. I just wanted to take some of the weight, if not all, off your shoulders. All of you women are always talking about being in your soft girl era. I thought that's what you wanted. I would never intentionally hurt you."

Leaning into him, I let the tears cascade down my face. I appreciated his concern. However, I was a big girl and could handle myself. Baron didn't fully understand me, and I didn't expect him to. There was a part of me he didn't know, and I preferred to keep it that way.

"Baby, tell me what's wrong? Did I hurt you?" Baron asked, attempting to console me.

I was an emotional wreck. It felt good to talk it out, but I still wasn't sure if things were going to change. Maybe I needed that time away in Houston to clear my head and figure out where I wanted this relationship to go. I sure as hell wouldn't get any clarity sitting in this house.

Baron lifted my chin and kissed my lips, pulling me from my thoughts. My pussy melted instantly in his embrace. Wrapping my arms around his neck, I reciprocated the energy by deepening our kiss. I needed this. A release would do my body justice.

Lifting my dress over my head, he pushed me toward the wall. Our kiss intensified as he dipped his fingers inside my panties. A soft moan escaped my lips while I moved my hips in a circular motion against his fingers.

"Damn, bae. Yo' shit wet as fuck."

"Ummm. Can you fuck me now?" I asked sexily. I wasn't in the mood for all that talking. I wanted the dick.

"Let me taste that pussy real quick."

Rolling my eyes, I threw my hands up dismissively. Baron wasn't bad in bed, but he couldn't give head for shit. Whenever I let him do it, he licked my pussy too hard, and that shit turned me off.

"You know what? Never mind."

Exhaling in frustration, I shoved Baron out of the way and stormed to the bathroom. Hot on my heels, he stopped the door with his foot before it could close.

"Chi, why the fuck are you always tripping? How did yo' crazy ass go from happy to sad to mad within an hour? I swear you be blowing me, man." It was true. I had gone through all those emotions within an hour. Maybe I was wrong, but I didn't care. Baron knew I hated oral sex with him. "You always ruining the mood and shit."

"I didn't ruin shit. Listen, we've been together for a while, and you know how I feel. How often do I have to tell you that you suck at giving head?"

"If I suck at eating pussy, why are you with me? It can't be that bad."

At that point, I felt like Baron was delusional. We'd had that conversation one time too many, and the fact that he kept asking was beyond me. There was no way I would lie about my feelings or fake moan like I enjoyed it when I didn't. Now that was what you called crazy. Every time we argued, he tried to flip it on me. We could've been having hot, sweaty sex. Instead, he chose to piss me off.

If I had access to my car, things would be different, and Baron knew that. Thank goodness I was headed to Texas with Royce because I needed a break. I wasn't completely innocent in the relationship. I knew I had some toxic ways. Sometimes Baron pushed my buttons, and I just lost control.

"I think you should go see a therapist," he suggested. Baron turned his back to me and walked out of the room.

"Nah, nigga, I need some dick," I shot back and slammed the bathroom door.

It was time for me to get ready for my trip anyway.

* * *

"Bitch, I thought it was hot in Georgia. This Texas heat is no joke. I can barely breathe," I complained as we walked out of the airport and to our Uber.

The driver helped us put our suitcases in the trunk while Royce tracked Alex's location.

"Can you believe this hoe told me she was leaving as she walked out the door this morning? She knew I wouldn't have enough time to get ready. I swear, if she's cheating, I'm done," Royce stated, shaking her head.

I couldn't believe how bent out of shape she could get about Alex. Her last nigga, Tommy, cheated on her, and she didn't say a thing. She simply blocked all communication and severed ties. This stalking Royce was a different person. I never actually expected her to do it when I suggested she invite herself.

"If she's been cheating, you need to beat her ass. Don't let her play in yo' face like that, cousin."

Royce gave me the side eye. "Why does everything have to resort to violence with you? I'm not doing all of that. If I have to subject myself to that type of behavior, then I need to walk away."

"Well, you're better than me." I chuckled.

I'm not saying Royce was wrong about how she felt. She wasn't rowdy like me. Shit, I had a lot of growing up to do, and I was working on myself one day at a time. Fighting was something I'd always done. Being from Chicago, it had to be like that. If you didn't stand up for yourself, you would get bullied, and Charae wasn't going for that.

If she found out somebody was messing with me at school, she would make me fight them when we got off the bus. Girls always liked to try me because I was one of the smartest in my class. By the time I reached high school, things had calmed down. I knew I wanted to go to Tilman, so I did everything to ensure I was on my best behavior. All that fighting shit came to a halt when I started taking my future seriously.

"I still can't believe I let you convince me to do this." Royce sighed.

Royce knew good and damn well, I hadn't influenced a thing. She claimed she wasn't the type to fight, but following Alex out of town was just as bad. Luckily, Baron hadn't given me a reason to think he was cheating. If he did, we wouldn't be together. Nobody wanted to feel insecure in their relationship.

We arrived at the Four Seasons Hotel in no time. The scenery was beautiful. I wanted to ask Royce how the hell she could afford this but decided to mind my business. Alex was doing well for herself and made sure Royce wanted for nothing. If she was cheating and brought another woman there, I'd be sick to my stomach. This wasn't the type of place you brought side bitches to.

The bellhop greeted us and took our luggage out of the trunk. We followed them inside, so we could check-in. My mouth dropped in awe at the extravagant fixtures and décor. After we checked in, we were escorted to the elevators.

"So, do we have to sneak around? You know, since Alex is here. I wouldn't want her to see us."

"Would you be quiet?" Royce whispered.

She didn't know I'd taken several shots of tequila since we landed. I was serious about spending some time alone away from Baron. For once, I felt like I could move around freely without him breathing down my neck. He always wanted to know where I was and who I was with. It had gotten to the point that I was starting to think he was the insecure one. It threw me off because we hadn't had those problems until recently.

I made sure to tip the bellboy since I had some extra cash. Even though Baron was against me going to Houston, he still gave me some money, so I could enjoy myself. When I left the house, we weren't on speaking terms, and I felt kind of bad for flipping out on him. Royce started unpacking as I stepped out into the hall to call Baron.

"Damn, I didn't expect a call from you so soon," Baron answered.

"Hey to you too. Listen, I didn't call to argue with you. I just wanted to apologize for how I reacted yesterday. I should've gone about that differently."

Instead of picking another argument like I expected, Baron accepted my apology. We talked for a few minutes as he expressed his concern for Byron. I chose to keep my mouth closed because I didn't want to get involved in their sibling drama. Baron and his parents needed to understand that Byron was going to do whatever he wanted, regardless of how they felt about it. He was only nineteen. Life was just getting started.

"Yeah, I understand how you feel. I know you only want the best for him, but sometimes you have to let people learn things for themselves. He'll be alright," I assured him.

I'd listened to enough of Byron's phone conversations. All he cared about was fucking bitches and hanging with his boys. I didn't mind having him around, but Baron seemed as if he wanted to be more of a father figure than a big brother. I understood his position, but Byron had a father. A prominent one at that. I liked Mr. Harvey, but it was that bitch Janice who I couldn't stand. She always had her snooty ass nose turned up, thinking I gave a fuck.

"You right, bae. I'm going to talk to him later. I need to see where his head is at."

"Okay. Just remember, Baron, you are his big brother, not his father," I reminded him before ending our call.

When I returned to the room, Royce had unpacked everything and was sitting on the bed with the remote in her hand. If she thought we were going to stay cooped up in that room, she had me fucked up. I didn't agree to come and stalk Alex. I came to enjoy myself.

"No, bitch, we are not about to do this." I sighed, taking the remote from her hands and turning the TV off.

"Chi, I was watching that!" Royce shrieked.

"Bitch, put your swimming suit on. A little sun never hurt anybody."

Royce's eyes grew wide as saucers. "You can go swimming. I'm not leaving this room."

"Fine, I'll go by myself." I shrugged.

That was on her if Royce wanted to waste her time sitting in the room.

Thirty minutes later, I sat poolside, sipping a virgin mojito while scrolling through social media. It was hot, but I'd adjusted quick. I sat under the canopy so I wouldn't get a tan. So far, the people had been friendly. A few older men had even volunteered to buy me drinks, but I declined. I understood many men liked big girls, but I wasn't into giving anybody the wrong impression. Plus, I wasn't sure if I was keeping this baby.

Even though I was on the thicker side, my body was still well-proportioned. It was both a blessing and a curse. Almost all my clothes had to be altered because my butt was big, and my waist was smaller. I'd been chubby all my life. Whenever I got into it with a bitch, the first thing they always called me was fat. I would be fat all day, but my face card never declined. My phone buzzed in my hand, alerting me of an incoming text from Arrington.

**We need to talk.**

That was where this bitch had me fucked up. The only reason she wanted to talk was that she knew whatever I had on Tracy was detrimental to that shop. She was right to think that because I was coming for her ass. She'd fooled everybody long enough. The gig was almost up. Instead of blocking her ass like I should've done a long time ago, I replied.

**I'll stop by the shop when I get back in town.**

Arrington was a pain in the ass, but if she wanted to talk, we could do that. If she wasn't talking about giving me controlling interest, then we didn't have shit to talk about. The only reason I'd been cool with not having a job was because I knew I'd be coming into ownership of the shop soon enough.

The only person who knew what I was planning was Royce. I'd been tight-lipped about everything until this point. I'd given those bitches grace when in all actuality, I should've taken everything. Just thinking about how terrible of a person Tracy had been made me sick. Suddenly, I wasn't feeling sitting outside in the sun. My temperature had risen, and I was in desperate need to be under air conditioning.

Grabbing my drink, I stood to my feet and collided with a tall, handsome specimen of a man. My drink hit the ground, the glass shattering on impact. Had he not reached out to hold my shoulders, I would've fallen into the pool.

"I-I'm so sorry. This hat must be blocking my view," I stuttered, mesmerized by his eyes.

"Maybe you need to take that big mothafucka off, so you can see where the fuck you're going," he harshly stated, taking me by surprise. His cold glare pierced through me as I stood there in bewilderment. Lost for words.

"You gon' move out the way or what, shawty? I ain't got all day to be standing here cus' yo' ass wanna be clumsy and shit."

Who the fuck was this nigga talking to? He looked like he was used to women letting him talk to them any kind of way, but I wasn't that bitch. If I wasn't going to tolerate that shit from my own man, I damn sure wasn't going to tolerate it from this nigga. I didn't care how fine I thought he was. That didn't excuse his rude behavior.

"First of all, I said I didn't see yo' goofy ass. Secondly, don't ever fix your lips to speak to me like that. I know ya mammy taught you better than that." I fumed.

The look on his face told me that he wasn't used to women matching his energy. Mr. Handsome flexed his jaw muscles as if he wanted to say something else but decided not to. Instead, he moved around me and coolly walked away.

If I wasn't hot before, I was hot now, and I could bet every dollar I had that the seat of my panties was soaked. Looking as good as he did should've been a crime. Shit, if he hadn't been so disrespectful, I probably would've flirted a little. That rude shit turned me off anyway. If this was how Texas niggas were, I didn't want any parts of it.

"Hey, did you enjoy the pool?" Royce asked when I returned to our room. Royce didn't give a damn about me enjoying the pool.

"No, I did not see Alex. Even if she was at the pool area, she wouldn't have noticed me with this big ass beach hat you made me wear."

"It's not that big. You're exaggerating."

"It's big as hell. I got up to come back inside and ran into this fine ass nigga."

"Did you give him your number?"

"Royce, I didn't come here to give my number to anyone. I'm with Baron, remember?"

Ignoring me, she continued to watch *Brat Loves Judy*.

"No. I literally collided with this man because of this hat. Dropped my drink and all."

"Are you serious?"

"Yeah, but even if I was single, I wouldn't talk to his rude ass. I had to curse him out for talking crazy."

"Chi, you can't be going off on random niggas. What if he had done something to you? I knew I should've gone to the pool with you."

"What were you going to do, Royce?" She wasn't a punk; she just wasn't one for confrontation.

"We would've jumped that nigga," Royce replied.

"That part." We laughed in unison.

Later that evening, Royce ordered room service, but I went downstairs to the bar instead. She had been tracking Alex all day, trying to figure out which floor she was staying on. She was trying her best to be discreet, but I knew it was only a matter of time before shit hit the fan. A week away from home sounded good, but I had a feeling shit would take a turn for the worse.

Baron and I hadn't talked since earlier. I was glad because I was tired of hearing about Byron. When I made it to the bar, I ordered myself a virgin daiquiri.

"How you doin' beautiful?" an unknown voice called out.

I rolled my eyes as I turned around to match a face to the voice. The man appeared to be in his late fifties. I knew exactly what type of time he was on. He was looking for a sugar baby. Unfortunately, I didn't have any sugar to give.

"Thanks for the compliment, but I'm not interested."

"At least let me buy you another drink," he offered, adjusting his tie.

I was trying to be nice, but I could no longer hide the agitation on my face.

"Unless you want to wear this daiquiri, I suggest you get the fuck on, Pop-Pop," I firmly stated.

I wasn't trying to come off rude, but I wasn't in the mood for fraternizing. I didn't give a damn if I was at the bar. Needing a drink didn't equate to being social. I hated when niggas assumed you were putting out just because you were sitting alone at a bar.

No sooner than Pop Pop moved from my line of vision, Mr. Handsome walked into the room with his mean ass. If we were going to keep running into each other, I needed to come up with a different name for him. His demeanor commanded the attention of every woman in the room, yet his eyes landed on mine. He continued to walk in my direction until he reached the bar. He ordered a double shot of Hennessey and turned in my direction.

"Fuck you looking at?"

*Was I staring at him the entire time?*

This nigga was really off the chain. Since the moment I ran into him, he'd been nothing but vile. The shit was weird because we didn't know each other from a can of paint. His life must've been miserable because there was no way he was this cold toward human beings.

"I'm looking at yo' crooked tie wearing ass," I shot back with attitude.

He looked down and adjusted his tie accordingly, causing me to burst into laughter.

"Yeah, I see you got jokes."

"There's more where that came from, rude ass. Bet you thought every bitch in here was drooling over yo' ass, didn't you?" I quizzed, taking another sip of my drink.

The bartender handed him his shot, and he placed a hundred-dollar bill on the bar. Without another word, he left the bar. Not only was he rude, but the nigga was also extremely arrogant and cocky. I didn't see how any bitch in her right mind would date him.

After finishing my drink, I decided it was time for me to go back upstairs to check on Royce. I knew she was in that room going crazy, trying to figure out what Alex was doing. This hotel was big enough that we probably wouldn't even see Alex. I went to pay for my drink and was informed by the bartender that someone had already paid my tab. When I asked her who, she pointed to the left toward none other than Mr. Handsome's mean ass. That wasn't what surprised me, though. Alex was standing next to him, along with some random bitch.

I couldn't believe this shit. This whole time, I'd been rooting for Alex, telling Royce that her cheating was all in her head when Alex was really there with another bitch.

Pulling out my phone, I called Royce and told her she needed to get her ass down there now. This was a nice establishment and all, but I would turn this bitch up if I had to. If Royce didn't want to smack fire from Alex, I would. Royce was too good of a person for Alex to be playing with her. She had us all fooled. I felt betrayed, like she was my bitch or something. Ten minutes later, I met Royce at the elevator.

"What took you so long to get down here?"

"I was packing my stuff, Chi. I told you if she was cheating, I'm done!" Royce cried.

See, that was the bullshit I was talking about. Royce was upset and in no condition to confront Alex and her little side-piece. However, I was. If Royce couldn't count on me for nothing else, she could count on me to slap a hoe.

"Chi, let's just go back upstairs and catch the next flight home. I just want to pack up my shit and have it out of the house before she returns to Atlanta."

"Absolutely not! We are about to go whoop this—"

"Royce? What the fuck are you doing here?" Alex questioned.

We'd been so engrossed in our debate that we hadn't noticed Alex or her sidekick, Mr. Handsome, approach us. While I was still trying to figure out how they knew each other, Royce rushed toward the elevators. I glanced over to the left and saw Alex's sidepiece walking in our direction. Alex attempted to grab Royce by the arm.

"Get the fuck away from me, Alexandria, with your cheating ass. You know I told you this was a deal breaker for me. How could you?" Royce cried.

"Bae, what are you talking about? I'm here on business."

"I guess you bring your side bitch to a fancy hotel to conduct business, huh?" All eyes landed on the unknown girl. If Royce would not address her, I would.

"Bitch, you have some nerve coming over here!" I spoke up. "Alex, I can't believe you."

By that time, I was ready to get shit popping. At that point, both Alex and her bitch could get it. Springing into action, I lunged at Alex but was grabbed from behind before my fist could connect to her face. Alex grabbed Royce and pulled her into the elevator, leaving me kicking and screaming for my life while being restrained.

"Put me down now!" I demanded. Mr. Handsome had all two hundred and fifty pounds of me lifted in the air.

"I'll put you down when you calm the fuck down, shawty. You out here trippin', and it's not a good look. See all these people with their phones out recording? If you don't want me to kill each and every one of them, I suggest you shut the fuck up and get yo' shit together," he whispered.

As I looked around, there were a few people recording and pointing in my direction. He could kill whoever he wanted; I didn't give a fuck. It was going to take a lot more than a threat to scare a bitch like me. I didn't know how they got down in Texas, but I stayed ready for whatever.

"Nigga, you don't scare me. I'm telling you right now, do what you gotta do."

Amongst those onlookers, I saw a familiar face in the crowd. I blinked several times to make sure they weren't playing tricks on me. It was *him*. The man I allowed to change the trajectory of my life within hours. My breathing became shallow, and my body became weak. I could feel the blood steadily pumping through my veins, but I felt lifeless. My chest began to heave in and out as I shook my head from left to right.

I hadn't seen him since that night. Every feeling and emotion that I'd suppressed started to resurface. I wanted to run and hide, but unfortunately, I was on full display.

"Please put me down. I can't breathe," I whispered, tears streaming down my face.

Mr. Handsome heard the panic in my voice and immediately put me down. His eyes scanned the crowd, attempting to figure out what had set me off. The room felt like it was spinning out of control as I struggled to regulate my breathing.

Falling to my knees, I started gasping for air. For some reason, I felt like a fish out of water. The last thing I remembered was his dark, piercing eyes burning a hole through my body.

\* \* \*

I woke up in a dimly lit room. My first instinct was to scream, but once my eyes adjusted, I realized I was inside our hotel room, but I didn't see Royce. I tried to remember the events leading up to me blacking out but kept drawing blanks. Sitting up, I rubbed my eyes and turned on the lamp next to the bed.

"What the fuck are you doing here?" I asked, taken by surprise. "Where's Royce?"

My eyes darted across the room. When I didn't see Royce's suitcase, I panicked. What had Alex's cheating ass done to my cousin? Why was her sidekick there? If he thought he was going to try something with me, he had shit twisted.

"I'm here because yo' ass started a bunch of shit last night."

What the hell was he talking about? I did what anybody would've done. It wasn't my fault Alex couldn't keep her tongue to herself. I didn't care what anybody said. I was going to ride for Royce, no matter what. She was more than a cousin to me. She was my best friend. I came to Texas to help her find out if Alex was cheating. The truth coming to light had nothing to do with me. This man trying to make it seem like everything was my fault was pissing me off.

I flung the sheets off my body and stared at Mr. Handsome. His haughty demeanor didn't make me feel afraid. He was definitely a man of importance. His aura screamed *that nigga*. All of that didn't matter because I couldn't stand his arrogant ass.

"Royce is fine. She's upstairs with Alex. They have asked not to be bothered until further notice."

I couldn't believe I let Royce convince me to come to Texas

with her, all for this to happen. Alex cheated, and Royce was probably in Alex's room laid up instead of flying back to Atlanta, as she previously stated.

After realizing I didn't have my phone, I contemplated my next move. My palms got sweaty as I wiped my forehead with the back of my hand. What was I supposed to do with that information? Sit there and look crazy. I think the fuck not.

"So, where do you come in? I didn't need you to stay the night in my room to tell me that. I could've figured shit out on my own. How do I know you're not a homicidal maniac?" I quizzed.

Last night, I remembered him telling me he would kill every person with a phone out recording us if I didn't calm down. Then, like a ton of bricks, it hit me. The powerless feeling had returned. My knees felt weak. Rubbing the back of my neck, I leaned against the door for support. The thumping in my chest felt like beating drums. My chest tightened as I struggled to breathe. I was sure Mr. Handsome thought I was crazy by now.

He coolly walked in my direction. Before I could protest, he pulled me into a hug. His embrace was reassuring, and at that moment, I felt like I was going to be okay. He rubbed my back and allowed me time to calm down until my breathing regulated. I was so embarrassed. How could I allow myself to be so vulnerable in front of him?

Gently tilting my head upward, he stared into my eyes. He was genuinely concerned. The tension slowly started to leave my body as he used his thumb to wipe my tears. I wanted to run and hide, but his other hand was on the small of my back. My body felt like it would melt into his. As if we'd become one. Who knew so much passion could be felt with a simple gaze. This was crazy. I had to get away from him.

Without warning, I wiggled free and ran into the bathroom,

slamming the door behind me. I leaned against the sink and prayed he would leave. There was no way I could face him again. He'd witnessed a side that I tried hard to suppress. I was exposed.

"Can you please just leave?"

"Not until you come out of the bathroom."

Arguing with this man was going to be pointless. Throwing my hands in the air, I slowly opened the door and stepped into his view. He sat in the lounge chair, peering out of the window. The skyline was beautiful, but I was in no mood to take it in. All I wanted to do was crawl into a hole and stay there. There was no need for me to be embarrassed now. He had witnessed me at my lowest, and there was nothing I could do to change that. I slowly walked over to the bed and sat down. The little energy I did have left had been depleted from my body.

"Last night, something triggered you. What was it?" His tone was low and firm.

He stood up from the lounge chair and walked closer until his tall frame towered over me. My heartbeat quickened, and for a moment, I thought I saw his eyes soften again. This man had witnessed me have a full-blown panic attack and had obviously been the one to bring me back to my room.

Why was he so interested in finding out what triggered me? It wasn't any of his concern, and I wasn't naïve enough to think he cared. I'd lived with this trauma for years, and there was nothing anyone could do for me. It was bad enough I was haunted by him in my dreams; I couldn't bear to face him in real life. I couldn't help but wonder if his presence had been a coincidence or if he'd been following me. Either way, I had to get the fuck out of there. I didn't want to risk the chance of running into him again. I wasn't strong enough.

"How do you expect me to talk to you about anything when

I don't even know your name? You've been nothing short of an asshole since the day I met you."

"Rylo," he answered.

I wondered if that was his street name. Rylo was dapper in a suit and tie, but I could spot a hood nigga from a mile away. Whatever the case, he cleaned up nicely. Rylo wasn't a man of many words. He stood in the same spot, patiently awaiting my answer. The silence between us was deafening, but I refused to talk about my personal life with a stranger.

"How do you know Alex?"

"That's my little sister. You don't need to know shit else. This ain't twenty-one questions."

That was exactly what I was talking about. This was my third encounter with him in two days, and he'd been nothing but an insolent bastard. He'd gone from consoling me to talking crazy in a matter of minutes.

The crazy part was that Royce nor Alex had ever mentioned her having a brother. I wondered if he was someone she was close to and considered a brother or if they were really related. I made a mental note to ask Royce about that. Even if I considered talking to Rylo, he'd just ruined it with his response.

"You know what? I'm not telling you shit. I wasn't going to anyway, but your attitude is unpleasant, and I don't see how anyone can stand to be around you. So, I'd appreciate it if you get the fuck out of my room," I fumed, pointing toward the door.

Fuck him. I didn't need shit from the nigga. His presence wasn't needed as far as I was concerned. Without another word, he left my room.

Sighing with relief, I found my purse and pulled out my phone. I needed to call Royce and curse her ass out since she thought it was okay to leave me with a stranger. She knew how I felt about being around random men I didn't know. I didn't care how long she'd known him. It was unacceptable. That man could've done anything to me.

"Hey, Chi." I could hear the smile in her voice, which left me confused.

Her girlfriend had cheated on her, and there she was, answering the phone all chipper like she'd hit the fucking lotto.

"Bitch, how the fuck did I wake up with Alex's so-called brother in our room? Royce, how could you?" I questioned as I wiped the lone tear that slid down my cheek. I was trying my best to keep my composure, but deep down, I was raging.

"I'm sorry, Chi. Rylo and Alex are blood, so I trusted him with you. So much happened in such a short time. I barely had time to react to the entire situation. Alex and I stayed in the room until about three this morning. What happened down there? What made you pass out like that."

Just like she had questions, so did I. All I remember was seeing him and falling to my knees. I didn't want to tell her who I'd seen because I wasn't too sure. It would sound crazy if he wasn't there. I'd never hallucinated, but I couldn't rule out the possibility.

"I don't know. I think maybe I just had a panic attack out of nowhere," I lied. "How did I get upstairs?"

"Rylo carried you after I assured the front desk that you were fine and didn't need medical attention. I think you blacked out."

"Well, what happened with the girl Alex has been cheating with?"

"That's a whole different story. I'll tell you about it when I get back to the room. Long story short, she wasn't cheating, but I gotta go. Alex just came out of the bathroom," she whispered, ending our call.

# Chapter 8
## *Rylo*

Chi was a piece of work, but there was something about her that I couldn't quite put my finger on. One minute she was in distress, and the next, she was forcing me out of her room. Usually, I didn't make it my business to care about what a bitch was going through, but the way shawty spazzed out last night was alarming. I needed to talk to Alex to see what she knew.

I went downstairs to get another room for myself since Alex and Royce were in my presidential suite. I made sure to get my room on the same floor as Chi, so I could keep an eye on her. It wasn't my job, but I felt sorry for her. Somebody in that crowd had done something to her. Either that or she was hallucinating. Once the receptionist handed me my room key, I went to the restaurant and ordered myself some breakfast. I had been up the entire night and had worked up an appetite.

"What was all of that about last night?" Taryn, Ronnie's wife, asked.

I hadn't realized she was standing behind me. Taryn and Ronnie had been married for nearly twenty years. They were in their early forties, but Taryn didn't look a day over twenty-five. If Ronnie wasn't my homeboy, I would've been hit Taryn. Not because I thought she looked good but because I knew she wanted the dick. I would catch her stealing glances when Ronnie wasn't paying attention, but I never entertained that shit. Outside of Alex, Ronnie had slowly started to gain my trust as I did his. I wasn't stupid enough to compromise that. Ronnie had been one of the biggest assets to my company, so keeping the partnership solid was a must.

"A lot transpired last night. I don't know all the details, so I can't speak on it. I do apologize for all the confusion."

It was true that I didn't know all the details because I hadn't talked to Alex yet. It didn't take much to figure out that Royce thought Alex was cheating. I told her she needed to be honest with Royce, but she assured me she had the shit under control. Taryn didn't need to know all of that, though.

"You don't have to apologize. I know what comes with this line of work. Ronnie has been in the same line of business since we got married twenty years ago. There were plenty of times when I thought he was cheating, so I followed him," she revealed. "I had to learn to start doing me." She winked.

"Ronnie still sleep?"

"No. He just got back from his morning jog. He'll be down shortly. Want to join us for breakfast?" She smiled coyly, touching my arm.

Taryn was a trip. She didn't care that we were out in the open. Anybody could've seen her, including her husband. My loyalty was with him, but I'd lay a nigga down if he thought he was going to approach me about a bitch. I didn't want to be mean, but I had to walk away before I said some rude shit.

"Nah, I'm good. Tell Ronnie I'll holla at him later."

Taryn was taken aback by my sudden curtness, but I ain't give a fuck about none of that shit. Ronnie needed to come get her ass.

When I got back upstairs, I made a few phone calls. I needed to push our scheduled meeting back a few hours, so I could be on point. After I ate my food, I took a shower and tried to get some rest, but I couldn't help thinking about Chi. It was fucked up that she was by herself and had obviously experienced some sort of trauma. I wasn't going to force her ass to tell me what she'd seen. If she wanted to be secretive, then she was on her own. I didn't know her, but Alex liked her, so she was good in my book, except for that smart ass mouth.

Later that evening, I was dressed and in the dining room, going over a few details with Ronnie before the meeting. I was grateful that Taryn decided to go to the pool instead. I felt like she had no reason to be involved in our business affairs, but Ronnie explained that he wanted the company of his wife. Business was business. Wife or not, some things went without saying. Which was why Alex left Royce's ass at home. We had no way of knowing that she was going to pop up. How she tracked Alex's location was still a mystery to me.

"Wasup, fam?" Alex greeted, dapping both of us up.

"Going over some details for this meeting."

Alex sat down as Ronnie airdropped keynotes for the meeting. Her presence wasn't a requirement. Much like me, she was overprotective and felt like I needed her there. I didn't mind because I trusted her with my life. Alex was the type to shoot first and ask questions later. By the time she was thirteen, I'd taught her how to use a gun, and she'd been on point ever since.

"Ronnie, you mind giving us a minute?"

Nodding his head, he rose from the table and went to the bar. After all that had transpired in the last twenty-four hours, I needed more than a drink. A nigga needed the whole damn bottle. Getting drunk would throw me off my square, so I opted for a shot or two.

"The fuck was that shit last night, sis?"

Alex closed her eyes and dropped her head.

"Man, this crazy ass girl thought I was cheating on her."

"I figured that much. Why yo' hardheaded ass ain't tell her what you was coming to Houston for?"

Alex had met with a distributor from the Columbian Cartel to negotiate the price of a new product. For the first time, I'd taken Pops' advice and allowed her to discuss business without my input. She had shit fucked up if she thought I wasn't sitting in on the meeting, and I'd done just that.

"It's not as simple as you think." Alex looked away as if she was struggling to find the right words. "Royce is different. She's ain't with all that shit." Sighing heavily, she put her dreads into a bun on top of her head.

"What you saying? She gon' leave you or some shit?"

Royce had been a constant factor in Alex's life for a while. When the two met, Alex was going through a difficult time, and Royce came along and changed that. Unfortunately, I hadn't found that, and I wasn't looking. I deserved to be alone. I'd done some fucked up shit in my thirty years. Nothing was off limits except killing women and children. I ain't rock like that.

"Shit, she might. I told her I came here to sit in on the meetings with you to start learning this side of the business. Since there's a business convention being held here this week, she believed it."

That much was true. I'd come to the business convention to network and gain a few potential clients I'd been scoping out. I would always have my sister's back, but I didn't like being involved in her bullshit. Alex tended to make shit harder than it had to be. Vouching for her wasn't a problem. What she didn't understand was that this situation had the potential to blow up as it had last night. Royce was a smart girl; she would figure out that Alex was involved with the Cartel sooner or later.

Alex and I talked for a few more minutes before I

summoned Ronnie back over to our table. The meeting was scheduled to start in the next ten minutes. My assistant, Mary, joined us and pulled out her laptop, a notepad, and a pen, so she could take notes. Alex excused herself from the table to use the restroom. A few minutes later, she texted to tell me she was getting food for Royce and Chi. My client was scheduled to arrive, and I couldn't keep him waiting by starting the meeting late. That was why wives and girlfriends needed to stay at home when it came to handling business.

"Well, if it isn't Mr. Ryan Lopez himself. I've heard many good things since the last time we spoke."

"Good to see you, man," I greeted as I stood up to shake his hand.

"I hope I'm not too late. They delayed my flight this morning," Sterling informed.

"It's all good. We were just getting started. This is my assistant, Mary. She will sit in with us today."

Sterling nodded his head before he presented a business plan to me.

Alex returned to the table, and I could tell she was pissed. Her eyes shot daggers in my direction as she listened to Sterling speak. She had stood firm on not wanting me to work with him. I couldn't honor her wishes if she refused to tell me why. He'd been thoroughly vetted by Ronnie, and his record was squeaky clean. On paper, I had no reason to deny him business. Especially when he'd presented me with an eight-figure proposal.

This would be one of my biggest investments to date. I wanted to make enough money through this business to retire and give Alex and myself the opportunity to step away from the drug game completely. Even though I had been working behind the scenes to keep my image intact, I was ready to give that shit up completely. Ever since Brandon died, my heart hadn't been in it.

"What the fuck, Rylo?" Alex fumed after the meeting was over.

"Fuck you expect me to do when you won't tell me the problem? Business is business. All that personal shit is irrelevant."

Alex's nostrils flared, signaling her anger. "Just know you just signed a deal with the fucking devil himself," she snapped as she turned on her heels to walk away.

Instead of chasing after her, I allowed Alex room to calm down. The last thing I needed was for her to act off emotion and cause a scene. At that point, I had grown frustrated. That was the only downside with Alex. She sometimes allowed her emotions to control her logic. After taking a few shots with Ronnie, I excused myself and headed upstairs to the presidential suite that I'd allowed Alex to take over. When I stepped off the elevator into the suite, I heard loud voices coming from the bedroom.

"No, I'm ready to go right now!" Chi yelled. Her voice had gone up several octaves.

"Chi, give us a chance to pack. You expect us to leave our stuff here?" Royce countered.

Alex walked into the living room, visibly angry. She rolled her eyes while grabbing various objects to pack into her suitcase. Chi came into the living room behind her and cut her eyes in my direction.

"Rylo, can you take Chi to the airport? She doesn't want to wait for us to pack our shit. Y'all shouldn't have brought y'all asses here anyway. Chi, I know it was your ass who put her up to this shit."

"It was a joke, and Royce ran with it. That's not my fault. I agreed to come here with Royce, so I could get away to relax. I didn't come here to spy on you. All I did was try to support my cousin. I'm sure you understand that. If not, I don't know what the fuck to tell you," she explained.

Alex was so pissed that she refused to look in my direction.

"Can y'all stop arguing with each other? It's done with. I shouldn't have made Chi come."

"Royce, I ain't two seconds off yo' ass either." Alex fumed.

"Well, if you weren't such a liar, I wouldn't have to go to these extremes."

"I'm ready to go!" Chi chimed in.

Shit, I was too. All this arguing back and forth shit was starting to make my head spin.

Without asking any questions, I grabbed Chi's suitcase and motioned for her to follow me.

"You coming, or you just gon' keep standing there lookin' crazy?"

Chi grabbed her purse and folded her arms across her chest. We stepped on the elevator and rode it down to the first floor. My security detail was already in the lobby waiting for me. I instructed them to take Chi to the car, so I could check out of my room. On my way out the door, I heard Sterling calling my name. He caught up to me as I approached the Black SUV that was waiting for me.

"Ryan, thanks for looking out. I promise you won't be disappointed," he said, shaking my hand once more.

"No doubt. We gon' get this money—"

"Bitch ass nigga!"

The next thing I knew, Chi was out of the truck, swinging on Sterling like a mad woman. Caught off guard, Sterling stumbled backward, pinching his nose. Before I had time to react, my security grabbed Chi from behind. Sterling started walking in her direction, and I sprang into action. Pulling out my gun, I pointed it directly at Sterling as Chi screamed all sorts of obscenities.

"Nigga, I'll kill you with my bare hands. You think I don't know Dion sent you? I hate you for what you did to me! I hope you rot in fucking hell, bitch. Yeah, I ain't scared of yo' bitch ass no more. Come get yo' shit rocked again, nigga!" Chi screamed.

She was rowdy, and that shit damn near made my dick hard.

"Step any closer, and I'ma blow yo' shit the fuck back."

By that time, I'd put two and two together. Sterling was who she saw last night. When we met this morning, he made it a point to say he'd just gotten off a flight. Whatever he had done to her, he'd caused a lifetime of trauma.

"Aye, man, this bitch tripping. I don't know her."

"Oh, so you don't remember that night when we were at a college party at Tilman, and you raped me? I know you didn't forget. You've ruined my life, and I hope the world sees you for the predator you are."

Sterling's eyes turned dark, and I knew Chi was telling the truth.

"What are you talking about? I haven't been charged with anything."

"That's because your bitch ass daddy is the dean."

I motioned for my security to put Chi in the truck. Sterling glanced at me, and I cocked my gun. I guess this nigga thought shit was sweet. No, I didn't know Chi at all aside from the few encounters we'd had over the past few days, but I refused to do business with a rapist. That explained why Alex didn't want me to do business with him.

"Ryan, she's lying. I promise I would never do something like that," he pleaded.

"Our business here is done, my nigga."

"You can't do this. You signed a contract."

"Boss, we gotta go."

I tucked my gun back in my waistband as I got in the truck

to a hysterical Chi. We drove off the hotel premises. I waited until we were away from the hotel and asked the driver to pull over. Chi was shaking while hyperventilating. I hopped out of the truck and walked around to the other side. Opening the door, I pulled Chi out and embraced her. I wasn't an affectionate type of nigga. Never been, but I couldn't just sit back and watch her go through this alone.

Just like this morning, I rubbed her back until her breathing regulated. She kept her head buried in my chest until she was calm. When she looked up at me, her eyes were red and puffy from all the crying she'd done. I knew what it was like to have a panic attack. I had one the night I found Brandon and hadn't had one since. I thought I was going to die standing there looking at his lifeless body. I could only imagine how Chi felt, having to face her assailant.

"I really appreciate what you did back there. I knew I wasn't crazy."

"Shit, it looked like you had him, Tyson," I joked.

A smile spread across her lips as I continued to hold her in my arms. By the time we realized what was happening, we both pulled away. Chi quickly got back in the truck, and I followed suit. I immediately made a phone call to have Ronnie obtain the security footage from the hotel. I couldn't have an image floating around of me pointing a gun at the mayor's nephew. Once I was done talking to Ronnie, I called Mary to have her charter a jet. I wasn't the type of nigga who flew commercial.

"Wow, a jet? What was wrong with you dropping me off at the airport?" I understood Chi didn't know who I was. I figured she was from Chicago, hence her name. Everybody in Atlanta knew I was the nigga to see. Shit, I'd made my first million by the time I was twenty.

"I'm going back to Atlanta. I'm not about to send you on a flight by yourself after what just happened."

"I didn't think you gave a fuck, with your mean ass."

"Don't think we cool after this. I'm dropping yo' ass off as soon as we land."

I ain't gon' lie. Each time I hugged Chi, I felt connected to her. I knew better than to keep in contact with her because I'd do nothing but hurt her. The day she bumped into me at the pool, I could tell she wanted a nigga. Chi was fine as fuck too. I had a weakness for brown skin females. Something about Chi made me want to eat her thick ass up, but I wasn't on that right now. Plus, her mouth was off the chain. If she did have a nigga, I was sure she gave him hell.

I needed to go back to Atlanta to see Mayor White anyway. Sterling's bitch ass probably called and let him know I'd pulled a gun out on him. It would only be a matter of time before he called me. Also, I needed to figure out how we missed the fact that Sterling was a sexual predator. Shit was crazy because there was too much pussy out in the world for niggas to be taking it. Bitches freely gave that shit away.

"That's fine. I don't wanna be around yo' rude ass anyway." She sneered as she folded her arms across her chest and peered out of the window.

Chi was in a daze. I could only imagine what she was thinking.

When we landed back in Atlanta, I offered to take Chi wherever she needed to go. We hadn't said two words to each other, and I wasn't tripping about that. I knew what it was like when you had no one to talk to, but I preferred it that way. Something told me it was different with her. Chi wanted to talk about what she was going through but probably thought no one would understand her.

I'd never been invested in what a female had going on outside of Alex, so this shit was new to a nigga. Something in me wanted to protect her mean ass. I could tell she'd never had that before. Then again, I could be wrong. I sent Ronnie a text, letting him know I wanted details on Chi.

"You can just drop me off at the nearest hotel. I'll figure the rest out from there."

Instead of asking her questions, I instructed my driver to pull up to a hotel nearby. I guess she would figure it out from there. I felt kind of bad about leaving her after what had just happened with Sterling. I wondered why she wanted to check into a hotel. What was she running from?

When we pulled up, I grabbed her luggage out of the car and carried it inside.

"I can take it from here."

I needed more information from her, but now was not the time. Something wasn't adding up, and since it involved Sterling, I was going to get to the bottom of it.

# Chapter 9
## *Arrington*

I woke up to several missed calls and messages from a few of my friends. I didn't even have time to open my eyes good before I received another call from Sydney. I started not to answer, but the way she'd been blowing me up let me know it was something important. Getting out of bed, I put my phone on speaker while stretching.

"This better be life or death, bitch. I was sleeping too good." I yawned.

My friends knew I didn't wake up early on my off days. When I first started doing hair, I made it a point to work on my off days just to boost my clientele. I learned the hard way early on that it was easy to burn yourself out working six days a week.

"You and Rylo broke up?"

"Girl, hell no. I wasn't playing when I said I wasn't coming up off that nigga. We locked in."

There was a long pause before she spoke again.

"Well, look at the video I just sent you."

Once the text came through, I told Sydney to hold on. At first, I couldn't make out what was going on. There was a lot of commotion in the background, but after a few seconds, Chi's face came into view. I found it quite odd because Sydney didn't know Chi, and if she did, there was no way of her knowing we were stepsisters. Just when I was about to ask Sydney how she knew Chi, Rylo's face came into clear view. I wasn't sure what had transpired for him to be holding her from behind and whispering in her ear. Immediately, my blood began to boil.

"What's going on, Arrington? That nigga cheating on you with a big bitch?"

I didn't have time for Sydney's shit. A part of me felt like she was jealous of my relationship with Rylo and couldn't wait to deliver the bad news. I swallowed the lump in my throat as I continued to watch the video. As if on cue, someone stepped in front of the camera, blocking the view. When they moved, Chi had her legs wrapped around my man while he carried her toward the elevator. All I saw was red.

"Let me call you back, Syd."

I tossed my phone on my king-sized bed and started pacing back and forth. Rylo hadn't called me in days, and I now knew why. He was busy fucking my stepsister. I'd called him every day, and he had yet to answer or return my phone calls. I'd feel different about the video if it was any other person but Chi. First, she wanted to steal my shop, and now she was trying to steal my man.

What bothered me the most was that I texted her yesterday, telling her we needed to talk. When she replied that she was out of town, I didn't think to put two and two together because I had no knowledge of the two knowing each other. Having never mentioned Chi to Rylo, the only person who could have introduced them was Royce. I tried to come up with logical reasons as to why she would go behind my back after I allowed her to work in my shop. I thought we were better than that. Then again, she didn't owe me any loyalty. I knew the bitch didn't halfway like me, but damn. Royce was a snake and would be dealt with accordingly. All the times I asked her to hang out or go on a double date, she always declined. Royce had been plotting, and at that point, she needed her ass beat.

I was so distraught; I could hardly focus. Rylo was everything I wanted in a man, but I couldn't get him to act right for some reason. I had never been the jealous type. However, this was a whole new level of hurt. I'd put in years with this man to secure my spot, and I'll be damned if I allowed another bitch to take it.

That explained why he had been adamant about us not being in a relationship. I knew one thing—they both had me fucked up. Rylo had only taken me to places that required him to have a date so he could look good. I mean, who wouldn't want to have a bad bitch like me on their arm? I enjoyed being with Rylo, but I hated those boring ass events. I had been practically begging him to go on a trip out of the country, and he always told me no. I didn't understand; it wasn't like he didn't have the money.

Picking up my phone, I contemplated whether I should call Rylo. There was a possibility that he wouldn't answer, which would further piss me off. Popping up to his house was out of the question. From what I'd heard, Rylo wasn't to be played with, and I wasn't trying to fuck around and find out. It was only a matter of time before he sent for me anyway. I would just have to wait until then.

Instead of getting up and getting dressed for the day, I climbed back into bed and cried my eyes out over a man who couldn't care less. Rylo was like a drug that I couldn't get out of my system. Even though he was an asshole, I learned to deal with him. We didn't have a title, but that didn't make it hurt any less.

I didn't mean to fall for Rylo; it just happened. At first, I took the situation for what it was. I saw an opportunity and jumped on it. I looked out for him, and he looked out for me. It was never supposed to be anything more. Now, I was embarrassed because I'd been telling all my friends we were together. Everybody knew Chi was my stepsister, so it looked much worse on her part.

After wallowing in self-pity, I rolled out of bed, forcing myself to take a shower. I had to get out of the house. If I stayed there any longer, I was going to suffocate. I changed into a pair of jeans with a Milano t-shirt and headed to the nearest bar to drown away my sorrows. It wasn't healthy, but I needed to numb the pain. There was a plan I had in motion which would be ruined if shit didn't work out between Rylo and me.

On the way, I made a slight detour. Fuck going to the bar to get drunk. Nothing good would come from that but codependency. A bitch wasn't trying to end up like the girls in the movies who turned crazy over a nigga. Well, maybe I was speaking too soon because I was about to stir some shit up. I'd be damned if I came second place in Rylo's life because of Chi.

A few minutes later, I pulled up to Ride Right for an oil change. My car needed maintenance, and I knew exactly who could get me right. All eyes were on me once I stepped out of my truck. I was used to it, though. I realized you couldn't do shit but stare when a bad bitch like me entered the room.

"Welcome to Ride Right. How can we help you today?" A short girl with glasses asked from behind the counter.

"Yes, I'm looking for the owner, Baron."

If Chi wanted to hit low, I was going to hit lower. I wasn't foolish enough to believe that Chi didn't know Rylo was my man. Royce had given her the rundown like she did everything else. If she wanted to play games with me, I was going to make sure her nigga knew what she was doing.

I'd never met Baron in person, but all of that was about to

change. The only reason I knew they were together was that the local news station did a segment on black-owned businesses, and his shop was featured. He'd taken a picture standing next to Chi, which happened to be in a news story. There were also a few occasions when Royce was on the phone with Chi, and I overheard her talking about Baron, so I knew they were still together. It was time to expose Chi for the lying, cheating bitch she'd always been. Seeing them break up was going to give me great satisfaction.

"He's busy with a customer. You can sit in the waiting area until he's finished," she advised.

"What you need, ma? Maybe I can help."

I looked up into the eyes of a younger man who was a spitting image of Baron. I knew he couldn't have been old enough to have a grown son, so I figured he was Baron's brother. He still had a baby face but was just as fine as Baron. The t-shirt he wore said 'Harvey Towing,' and I assumed they had a tow trucking business as well.

"I don't think you can help me on this one, baby." I smirked.

His eyes wandered over my body as he licked his lips. Even if he was my age, I was way out of his league. Niggas had to have bread to fuck with a bitch like me.

"You never know, baby. Try me." He flirted.

"Byron, what I tell you about flirting with the customers?"

Baron came to the front, and I almost choked when I saw how fine he was in person. His stride exuded confidence as he walked behind the counter. My mouth agape, I stared at him intently. He wasn't topping Rylo, but the nigga looked good as fuck. I couldn't believe he liked big bitches. Well, I guess everybody had a type. Somebody had to love them.

"Baron, I know you're busy, but she has requested to speak with you," the receptionist stated, pointing in my direction.

Baron looked up, and we locked eyes. I didn't know what it

was about him, but he had this inviting energy surrounding him. Looking away, I pulled my phone out of my purse, preparing to show him the video of his precious Chi. That bitch probably had him thinking she was perfect. If he did, all of that was coming to an end today.

Baron stepped around the counter and offered me his hand to shake.

"How you doing? I'm Baron. The owner of the shop." He was polite in his approach, unlike Byron.

"I'm Arrington. Nice to meet you," I replied, shaking his hand.

"What brings you in today?" he quizzed, glancing at my truck.

"Umm, actually, I was hoping we could talk in private."

Baron's eyebrow rose a bit as he ushered me into his office. It wasn't much to look at. His desk had papers strewn across it, and there were multiple car parts in each corner of the room. If Baron was my man, I'd have his office clean and smelling good. He offered me a seat in the chair in front of his desk, but I stood instead. Everything in there appeared to be dirty with oil stains, and I didn't want to mess up my clothes.

"How did you hear about us?" The million-dollar question.

I hadn't thought about how I was going to approach the situation. Would he think I was crazy for tracking him down to let him know Chi was cheating? I guess we would have to find out. I was already there, and there was no turning back now.

"A news story I saw. It's a funny story. So, I'm not sure if you've ever heard of me, but I'm Chi's stepsister."

Baron's brows furrowed in confusion. He was mentally scanning his memory bank, attempting to piece things together. I didn't give a fuck if he told Chi about me being there. Once I dropped this video in his lap, that would be the least of his concerns.

"Now that I think about it, she has mentioned you a time or two."

"I'm sure they were all good things," I joked.

He shrugged as he sat on the edge of his desk. "I wouldn't say that. If you're not here to get your car serviced, then what brings you in, Arrington?"

Now we were getting somewhere. I knew Chi talked shit about me. She hated my guts, and I made sure she knew the feelings were mutual. The difference was that I didn't speak on her to my man. I watched in delight as Baron's eyes roamed my body. Chi must have benefited him in some other way because, clearly, we were two different women. I was damn near every nigga's fantasy.

"I came across this video on social media this morning," I replied, shoving my phone into his hands.

Baron watched the video in its entirety before handing the phone back to me. He appeared to be deep in thought but said nothing. A hint of sadness flashed across his face. The feeling was unsettling. I knew because I'd just experienced it hours before.

"What are you gaining by showing me this video?"

What the fuck did he mean? Baron was trying to be nonchalant, but I knew he cared. From what I understood, he was taking care of the household while Chi sat around doing nothing. Little did Royce know, I listened to her conversations often. Mainly, I wanted to know if Chi had said anything to Royce about taking ownership of the shop.

"You think I'm showing you this because we don't like each other?" I questioned, throwing my head back in laughter. "I'm showing you this because I wanted to let you know you're fucking with a treacherous bitch. That's my man in the video. It's crazy that she has that much hate for me. I mean, we don't get along, but I still love her. That's my sister." I don't know how I did it, but I mustered up a few tears.

"Damn, I ain't know that."

I was done there. Long as he knew about the sneaky bitch, my mission was complete. Baron could do what he wanted. It was out of my hands. After careful consideration, I figured it would be best if I didn't say anything to Rylo. I knew bringing Chi up would set him off, and that was the last thing I wanted. Rylo had this thing where he wouldn't call or pick up the phone if I pissed him off too bad.

"Now you know," I snapped before sashaying out of his office.

An hour later, I pulled up to my mother's house tipsy. I'd had a few drinks and should not have been driving, but I had to give her this tea in person. She hadn't said anything else to me about Chi and the shop, so I assumed things were still under control.

"I went to see your father," she said, coming down the stairs.

"You didn't tell him about Chi, did you?"

"No, but we need to get in front of this. She's probably waiting until he comes home. We need to be prepared. If Chauncy believes her, he's going to give her that shop. I knew I should've kept him out of the deal."

Years ago, when she started the shop, Mama asked for Chauncy's permission to use the rest of the money he had stashed to start her own business. He agreed to it with one stipulation—he wanted to be part owner, so he would have something to come home to once he was released from prison.

"Is there something else going on that I don't know about?"

119

Mama had her back turned to me, so I wasn't able to gauge her expression.

"No, sweetie, I've already told you how vindictive Chi is. You know that girl is crazy and needs to seek professional help. She's been walking around unhinged for far too long."

She was right about that. Chi had been a little off for as long as I could remember. She would get so angry to the point where she lashed out or resorted to violence. I stopped calling her crazy the day she threw a Barbie Jeep at my head for teasing her. To this day, I still have a scar on the left side of my forehead.

"Chi is sleeping with Rylo," I blurted out unintentionally.

At that point, I was desperate to get it off my chest. I refused to talk to my friends about it because they were under the impression that things between me and Rylo were smooth. Although it was tiring, I still had an image to uphold.

"She's doing what?" Mama quizzed as I pursed my lips together while nodding my head. "How do they even know each other?"

"Royce."

"She needs to be fired immediately. If I were you, I would whoop her ass."

Fighting Royce in the shop would only bring negative attention my way, and I wasn't trying to jeopardize my clientele. I'd been professional since the day I stepped foot in that shop, and I wasn't going to allow Royce to change that. I was going to make sure she regretted introducing them.

"As soon as she comes back from her little trip, she can kiss her job goodbye." I exhaled.

I was truly hurt about Rylo and Chi fucking me over. I didn't deserve to be treated like a second option.

"Good. You can stay here if you want, but I have somewhere to be," Mama said, grabbing her purse and heading toward the door. She stepped into a pair of Christian Louboutins and fixed her blouse.

"Those shoes are cute. Where you going?"

"To mind the business that pays me. See you later, baby," she said as she grabbed her purse and left.

I waited until Mama pulled out of the driveway and hopped in my truck. Something was up with her, and I was going to find out. My headlights were off as I followed her. Once she got onto the highway, I allowed several cars to get between us. I didn't want to risk the chance of her seeing me. I felt crazy following my mother, but she'd left me with no choice. I'd given her several opportunities to tell me what was going on, and she kept lying. Now, I had to play Nancy Drew.

It was at least forty minutes before she got off on the exit for Covington. Maybe she was going on a date. For ten years, she'd claimed to have been faithful to my father, but I knew better. I understood she had needs, but why be so secretive about it? It wasn't like I was going to tell anybody.

I slowed down as she turned into a parking lot. Pulling over, I sat on the side of the road, so she wouldn't see me. There was a black SUV parked on the side of the building. She got out of her car and approached the truck. The driver got out of the car and nodded his head at Mama. She returned a smile as he opened the back door.

The first thing I saw was a pair of Ferragamo's hit the pavement. So, I was right about one thing. She was indeed going to see a man. There was nothing to see beyond that point. I felt like I'd violated her privacy for nothing. I put my car in drive, preparing to pull off, but came to a halt when the mystery man's face came into view. My eyes almost bulged out of my head once I realized it was Mayor White. What the fuck were they doing meeting up, and how did she even know this man?

# Chapter 10
## *Baron*

Chi was coming home soon, and I wanted to take her somewhere nice. We'd been at odds for the past few weeks, and I wanted to make it up to her, mainly because a nigga was feeling guilty for fucking with Taina. I'd watched that video over and over but still didn't want to believe that Chi had been cheating on me. She hadn't mentioned another person going on the trip with them, but I was sure there was a logical explanation. I couldn't just jump to conclusions. I would simply ask. If she lied about it, then we would have a problem.

That was one reason I didn't like her hanging around Royce. Her ass was sneaky, and I didn't like that shit. I wouldn't be surprised if Royce set the shit up. Either way, I was going to find out.

Arrington was a whole different story. Whenever she spoke about Chi, I could see the hate in her eyes. Chi never talked much about her, but when she did, she made it very clear that they didn't fuck with each other. I had never met Arrington a day in my life, and for her to track me down to show me a video was odd. I made a mental note to ask Chi about their history.

Something wasn't adding up. It was like she wanted me to say something bad about Chi to fuel her fire. I pulled out my phone and dialed Chi's number.

"Hey, babe."

"Everything okay? You sound like something is bothering you."

"I'm fine. Just a little tired." She sighed.

"I can't wait to see yo' fine ass. I got something nice planned for you."

"Aww, Baron, that's sweet of you. Can I call you right back? I haven't eaten anything all day. I need to order room service before the kitchen closes."

"We haven't talked all day. Have Royce order it," I suggested.

It seemed like she was trying to rush me off the phone, and I ain't like that shit. I tried to listen to see if I heard any other voices in the room. There was some shuffling going on, but that was it.

"I thought you and Royce got a room together. They ain't got you feeling like the third wheel, do they? I'll come fly out there to keep you company."

"Just say you miss me, Baron. I'll be home tomorrow anyway." She chuckled.

"You already know I miss you. So, what, you just been tagging along with Royce and her bitch?"

"Baron, if you're asking if somebody else is on the trip with us, the answer is no. You really need to stop being so insecure. It doesn't look good. That's why you always want me to stay in the house."

"That's not true."

"Let me call you back, so I can order this food," she said and hung up in my face.

I knew Chi well enough to know that she was lying, and

that fucked me up. It wasn't like she knew about Taina or any other bitch I fucked. The way I saw it, we were equal. If she thought another nigga was going to take care of her while she sat at home, she was mistaken. Most niggas couldn't do that unless they were in the streets. It was all good. I was going to chill with Taina after I left the shop anyway. At least she was grateful to have me around.

After I finished up my last car for the day, Byron pulled up in his tow truck. He didn't have a car, so his truck was his only means of transportation. We hadn't seen each other lately because he had a lil' chick he was fucking with. Knowing Byron, that shit was only going to last for a couple of weeks until he got tired of the girl.

"Sup, bruh." Byron dapped me up. He smelled like a whole ounce of weed.

"Shit, bouta go get some food after I finish up here. What you got goin' on?"

"I'm glad you asked." Byron went to his truck and grabbed an oversized duffel bag.

I knew Byron well enough to know that whatever was in that duffel bag was trouble. Whatever he was up to, I didn't want no parts in it. He smirked as he unzipped the bag, exposing crisp one-hundred-dollar bills.

"What the fuck you doin' with all of this money, Byron?"

"Aye, man, calm down. It ain't nothing like that. My nigga Romeo wanted me to bring this here to stash it until he ready for it," he stated with a serious expression.

Byron was out of his mothafucking mind if he thought he was stashing drug money at my shop. I couldn't believe this nigga had the balls to ask me some shit like that. That was why I had second thoughts about the location of the shop. I got such a good deal that was hard to pass up, though. At the time, it was all I could afford.

"It wasn't a question, bruh. You know this his block." I didn't give a fuck if the block belonged to Obama. This nigga wasn't stashing shit at my shop. "Where you want me to put it?"

"Man, you and Romeo got me fucked up. Ain't no nigga telling me what I gotta do. Fuck out of here, fam. I'm not doing it. You can tell that nigga if he got a problem, he can come see me," I said, patting my chest for emphasis.

"I shouldn't of asked you. I ain't tryna put you in no shit, but my back is against the wall," he revealed.

He placed the duffel bag back in the truck. Surprisingly, he didn't argue me down.

That was why I told Byron to stay out of the streets. I'd heard of Romeo before, but the nigga didn't put no fear in my heart. I sold my weed here and there, but lately, I hadn't even been doing that since my plug got arrested.

"Take that shit back to that nigga and tell him you can't do it."

Once Byron left, my ringing phone pulled me out of my thoughts. When I pulled it out of my pocket, Chi's picture flashed across my screen. Instead of answering, I let the call go to voicemail. She wanted to be cute and hang up, so her ass could talk to my voicemail.

Once I closed the shop, I drove over to Taina's. Since the night we ran into each other at the gas station, we'd been hanging out a few times a week. Shit was crazy because things with us didn't end on bad terms. At the time, we were just at two different places in life.

"Hey, Bear!" She beamed with excitement as she opened the front door.

We embraced as we did every time we saw each other.

Taina had a nice house that had been recently built from the ground up and drove a Mercedes. I couldn't help but think that this was how our life together was supposed to play out. We used to sit up all night and talk about our dreams, and now we were both living them, just in two separate worlds.

"We can chill upstairs in my room. I was just about to turn on a movie."

The moment I walked in, I already knew what shawty was on. I'd spent the night with Taina almost every night since Chi had been out of town. She lived alone with her one-year-old, so I didn't have to worry about getting caught up. I damn sure wasn't going to let Taina spend the night at my house. Fucking with Taina wasn't the problem, but I knew if I kept this up, leaving her alone would be the hard part.

"You smell good, ma," I complimented, following her up the stairs.

"Thanks. It's the same perfume I've always worn." She turned around and smiled.

When we got to her bedroom, I kicked off my shoes and placed my phone on the nightstand. The TV displayed Netflix, but we wasn't on no chill shit. Taina looked good in her sports bra and boy shorts. Her ass sat up just right—had a nigga ready to dive in her shit face first. Since Chi was coming home tomorrow, I wasn't doing all that extra shit.

Taina walked up on me and wrapped her arms around my neck. We started kissing as I pulled her bra over her head, exposing her breasts. My lips grazed her nipples, causing a soft moan to escape her lips.

"I missed you today, Bear," she cooed as she dropped to her knees and unbuckled my pants. I sat down on the bed and allowed her to do her thing.

This was the type of shit I could get used to. Instead of popping off at the mouth, Taina was ready for a nigga. The only thing I was missing was a hot meal. Chi cooked, but she always had a problem when I ate at my parents' house. They loved Taina, so her being there with me had never been a problem.

My phone buzzed on the nightstand, displaying Chi's face. Before I had time to react, Taina hopped up and grabbed the phone. She slid her finger across the screen as if she was answering the call, and I almost punched her ass in her face. Snatching the phone, I pushed Taina away from me as I pulled my pants back up. Her eyes grew wide with fear. I was pissed, but not enough to put my hands on her.

"The fuck is wrong with you?"

"I was just playing, Bear. You know I wouldn't answer your phone."

"Ion play those types of games, Taina. Tell that shit to somebody else."

I grabbed my shit and headed downstairs with Taina hot on my heels. At that point, I didn't give a fuck about shit she was talking about. If she wanted somebody to play with, she could play with her baby daddy. I knew I was fucking up, and I wasn't trying to put Taina in a fucked up situation. But, honestly, if she answered the phone, she would be doing it to herself. Chi was rowdy and would be ready to beat my ass if she found out about Taina.

"I've seen her before," Taina blurted out as I opened the door. I turned around to face her to read her expression. "She came to the hospital a few weeks back and found out she was pregnant. Why didn't you tell me, Baron?"

Chi wasn't pregnant. Taina had her confused with someone else. If she'd gone to the hospital, I would know. The only place she'd gone to was the grocery store, and that was it. There was no way Chi was pregnant and hadn't told me. The last time I checked, it was impossible for her to have kids.

"I didn't tell you because she's not pregnant. Don't you think I would know that? I don't have a reason to lie."

Taina placed her hands on her hips and shook her head. "I don't think we should see each other anymore. Her being pregnant only complicates the situation. We should stop while we're ahead before someone gets hurt."

She didn't have to tell me twice. Although Chi wasn't pregnant, I refused to chase after Taina again. We'd been down that road before, and I'd grown since then. That part of my life was behind me. Even though a nigga was dead ass wrong, I still wanted to build with Chi. I got in my car and lit an already rolled blunt. Now that I thought about it, I needed to take my ass home anyway.

Once I made it home, I went to the kitchen and poured myself a shot of Patron. The house was quiet, so I went upstairs and knocked on Byron's door. When he didn't answer, I realized he wasn't there and was probably out running the streets. Shit, I was cool with having the crib to myself. I needed some time to get my mind right before Chi returned anyway.

After I took a few shots, I went into the bedroom and thought I smelled Chi's perfume. I checked the adjoining bathroom to make sure I wasn't tripping. She wasn't due to come back until tomorrow afternoon, and I planned to have the entire house decorated with flowers, balloons, and some of her favorite gifts. Once I was done taking a shower, I hopped in bed and drifted off into a deep sleep.

The next morning, I was at the shop bright and early. I only planned to be there for half the day, so I could run a few errands before Chi got off the plane. I was supposed to pick her up, but Royce volunteered to bring her home instead. This would be the only time I left the shop early because I hadn't been having a steady flow of customers like I was used to.

With the shop struggling, I needed to find a new plug to sell my weed on the side. Maintaining the household would be easier once things picked up. Since I was in a financial bind, I considered getting a loan from the bank. The only issue with getting a loan was not being able to pay it back. Asking my father had crossed my mind, but I didn't feel like getting a lecture. He was thorough in all his business dealings.

Byron pulled up to drop off a car for me to look at. Lately, I had been relying on his truck to bring in clientele. We hadn't talked since last night when he came in there, demanding I stash some money. At that point, I started to think the nigga wanted to be dead or in jail. He got out of the truck and did his visual inventory around the garage. He glanced at the transmission and shook his head.

"Stop playing with that girl and put the transmission in her car." Byron shook his head and laughed.

"I'll put it in, eventually. I have other cars that need to be worked on from paying customers."

Byron had some nerve showing up there, asking me about Chi's car. I was sure she put him up to asking me since I wouldn't give her a direct answer. Even though I agreed to her going to Texas, the shit still pissed me off. Everything revolved around what Royce wanted to do.

"Nigga, you have had that girl's car sitting in this shop with the part for two months. You so busy trying to control the girl that you don't realize you're pushing her away."

With relationships, Byron didn't know shit about how to treat a woman. Call it what you want, but I wasn't taking no advice from a nineteen-year-old still running the streets like a little ass boy. Byron had overstepped his boundaries for the last time.

"Look, don't tell me how I should treat my girl. We good."

"Shit, I can't tell. You out here looking like a simp trying to take care of Chi when she never asked you to. That girl is miserable sitting in that house. The only reason she hasn't been looking for a job is because she doesn't have her car, nigga. But you knew that already."

All this came from somebody who fucked random bitches he met in my shop. There was no way in hell I would ever take advice from his ass. If providing for my household and taking care of my woman made me a simp, then so be it.

"I don't take advice from niggas who don't have their shit together. You need to be worrying about your tow trucking company, so you can find a place."

"Now, a nigga needs to find a place. What happened to you being my big brother and taking as much time as I need? Nigga, you ain't doing this shit off the strength of me. You did it to look good, fam."

"Why you so pressed about it anyway? You fucking her or something?"

Byron looked at me as if I had two heads sprouting from my shoulders.

"Hell nah, but you better be careful because another nigga might come and swoop her up. She already talking about how you can't eat pussy." Byron smirked.

"Fuck you, nigga!"

I couldn't believe Byron thought I was helping him out to make myself look good. I'd been through hell and high water trying to get the lil nigga on the right path. That only made me realize I couldn't do the work for him. He had to want it for himself. Shit, the nigga didn't even do his own laundry. If he couldn't carry his weight, then he could bounce. I didn't want to put him out on the street, but he was starting to feel himself a little too much.

Then, this nigga was talking about me trying to control Chi. It wasn't that; I just wanted her to play her position. Not only that, but I met Chi in the strip club. She approached me first, and it was clear she knew what she wanted. At first, I didn't mind, but now I was starting to see that she wasn't changing.

When Chi made it home, I was going to talk to her about all this shit. Especially with Taina telling me she was pregnant. If she was, I wanted a paternity test. One thing I wasn't gon' do was take care of another nigga's baby. That was out of the question.

Another thing that alarmed me was her erratic behavior. One minute she was happy; the next, she was either crying or angry. Then there were the panic attacks. I'd tried everything I could to be there for her because I knew what she'd been through.

It was a little after noon, and I had just gotten back from copping a Chanel bag for Chi. I got some balloons and flowers and put rose petals all over the house. A nigga went all out too. I had her favorite wine along with some fruit, so she could take a bubble bath. I wanted to ask Chi about that other nigga but decided to leave that where it was. I couldn't trip on her when I knew what I was out there doing behind her back. I was done with Taina. We'd moved on from each other, and it needed to stay that way.

Once I finished setting everything up, I sent Chi a text to see where she was. Her plane should've landed over an hour ago, but knowing Royce, she probably had Chi going somewhere across town. Before I set my phone back down, I heard a knock on the door. Chi was right on time. I wondered why she didn't use her key, but then again, she was probably carrying a lot of stuff.

I swung the door open and was face to face with the barrel of a gun. Immediately, I threw my hands up. As I slowly backed away, two armed men barged into the apartment and closed the door behind them. The first thing I thought about was Chi. What if she walked in with these niggas pointing a gun to my head? I prayed she wasn't close.

"Look, man, I ain't got shit in here. Take whatever y'all want."

One of the niggas started looking around the living room while the other kept the gun trained on me. Weighing my options, I thought about trying to run out the front door, but I knew they would shoot me if I did that. The only option I had was to let them search the house. It didn't make a difference because I didn't have shit they were looking for.

"Where the fuck is that nigga Byron? He said my money is here."

I thought back to last night when Byron tried to convince me to stash Romeo's money. I'll be damned if this nigga didn't find my house and run up in my shit. If Byron had run off with Romeo's money, I was going to fuck him up.

"Nigga, I already told you, ain't shit here."

Next thing I knew, the butt of the gun came crashing down on my head several times. I stumbled backward, landing on the couch.

"It ain't at that raggedy ass shop either. You told Byron if I had a problem to come see you, right? I'm here, nigga. Fuck you gon' do, my nigga?"

"Nah, man, I don't know what you're talking about." He walked back over to the couch where I was sitting and hit me with the butt of the gun for the second time.

Blood trickled down my face as I tried to apply pressure to my head. The other nigga had ransacked the entire apartment within minutes.

"Ain't shit up there."

Romeo peered in my direction with a mug on his face. I

didn't know how much more of him hitting me with the gun I could take. He'd already busted my head wide open. The only thing left for him to do was torture or kill me.

"I'ma ask you a question, and I want you to think about it long and hard before you answer. I would hate to have to kill you, Baron. Where is Byron?"

"I don't know. I haven't talked to him since earlier."

"Wrong answer." Romeo laughed as he pointed his gun at me and let off two shots.

# Chapter 11
## *Chi*

The day had finally come for me to return home, and I should've been relieved, but I wasn't. Spending time alone was something I never knew I needed until now. Royce was on her way to pick me up, and I couldn't wait to stop and get something to eat. All that cooking shit I'd been doing before was dead. This pregnancy had me craving French fries, and as cute as it sounded, that was about to come to an end as well. I

Last night when I tried to call Baron back, he didn't answer his phone. At first, I thought he was sleeping, but something told me to go to the house to check and see if he was there. The whole Uber ride, I battled with myself on if I should go. I had already talked myself into it, and there was turning back.

I went inside, thinking that Baron was asleep since he hadn't answered the phone. My heart dropped to my feet when I realized he wasn't there. It was two in the morning, and Baron never stayed out late. The only explanation was that he was somewhere cheating. What sealed the deal was when I found a pack of condoms with one missing on the dresser. I didn't want to believe he was stupid enough to fuck another bitch in my house. Baron already knew how I got down. After searching all the trash cans and the toilet, I was kind of relieved that I hadn't found the wrapper for the missing condom.

Now that I knew he was fucking around, I was going to move accordingly. My feelings were hurt because I thought he was different. Baron never gave me a reason to feel like he was cheating. Even when we argued, he always made up for it. There was no way I was bringing a baby into this toxic mess.

After careful consideration and hours of crying my eyes out, I decided to get an abortion. Good thing I hadn't told Baron because I knew he would give me a hard time. I wasn't doing it because I was bitter. However, I didn't want to raise my child in a single-parent household. If I was going to have children, I wanted to do it the right way.

Grabbing my suitcase, I scanned the room to make sure I had all my belongings. Once I got down to the lobby, I checked my phone and saw that I had a missed call and a text from Baron asking where I was. The nerve of this nigga. At that point, he didn't get to ask me questions. Our relationship was over. The only part that pissed me off about the situation was that I'd put him on the lease, and I couldn't just kick him out without a fight.

"You shouldn't be walking with your face in the phone. Never know who's watching," a familiar voice stated.

Looking up from my phone, I stared into Rylo's piercing eyes. What the fuck was he doing there?

"Yeah, I'm from Chicago. Learned that a long time ago. Didn't anybody ever teach you to mind your business?" I questioned as I started walking away.

Rylo was sexy, and I couldn't help but notice how muscular his frame was. He wore regular clothes instead of a suit and tie.

His beard was neatly trimmed, and his long dreads looked freshly twisted as they flowed down his back.

"I need to talk to you about Sterling," he said as he followed me.

Stopping dead in my tracks, I turned around to face him.

"There's nothing to talk about. He raped me, and I got kicked out of school because I stabbed him. End of story."

His asking about Sterling only flooded my memory of that painful night. I tried my best to stay sane. Every time I thought about Sterling, which was daily, I wanted to kill him. He was the reason I'd purchased a gun in the first place. From that point on, I vowed to protect myself because nobody else was going to do it. The next nigga who tried to violate me was getting his brains blown the fuck out. I meant that from the bottom of my heart.

"Listen, I'm not trying to make you relive that night. I'm just trying to help you," he assured, as if he'd read my mind.

I appreciated the gesture, but I could handle myself.

"No, you listen. I was fine before you came along, and I'll be fine after. I don't need your help."

I didn't understand what he benefited from so called helping me anyway. Yes, he was Alex's brother, but that was all I knew about him. The fact that he had money probably impressed a lot of bitches but not me. I didn't know his status, but any man who could charter a jet with a single phone call was paid.

"Sterling is a dangerous man, and he'll come after you," Rylo countered.

My goodness, this man was so fucking fine. My brain was telling me one thing, but the look in his eyes had softened once again. Maybe he was being genuine after all. Still, my pride wouldn't allow me to accept. I hoped this nigga wasn't trying to scare me when he said that Sterling would come after me. Honestly, I'd feared him for years, and I was done allowing him to have that power over me. That was one reason I was able to muster up the strength to run up on his ass. Years of pent-up anger had fueled me. When I saw him walking out of the hotel with Rylo, I thought I'd been set up. It wasn't until Rylo pulled out the gun on Sterling that I realized he didn't know anything.

"Hey, what are you doing here?" Royce asked as she walked into the lobby.

"I came here to talk to Chi," he replied, his cold gaze returning.

"Well, have you talked to Arrington? She keeps calling me. Apparently, there's a video circulating on social media of you carrying Chi over your shoulder," she said, folding her arms across her chest.

"Arrington? You know her?" I quizzed.

Fuck the video. I wanted to know the tea. He wasn't required to tell me about Arrington, but somebody should've.

"Yes. I don't think they're together, but he definitely knows her," Royce stated.

That was news. We'd been out of town with this man for days, and I had no idea he was fucking with Arrington. What were the odds? Now I understood what people meant when they said Atlanta was small. The last thing I needed was for Arrington's man to be all up in my face. I didn't need her thinking I was trying to steal her nigga.

"Man, it ain't even like that."

"Then what's it like?" Rylo closed his eyes and dropped his head, which confirmed everything. "I understand you think Sterling is dangerous, but it's not for you to worry about. Like I said before, I don't need your fucking help," I snapped as I dragged my suitcase to Royce's car.

Once we were in the car, I broke down crying. I hadn't told anyone about Baron cheating because the wound was still fresh. Plus, Royce knew me better than anybody, and if I told her about Baron, she wouldn't take me home. My worst fear was catching him in the act.

"Cousin, what's wrong? You and Rylo didn't do anything, did y'all?"

Wiping my face, I gave her the side eye.

"Girl, no. He was already in the lobby when I came down. At first, I thought he came with you, but when I didn't see your car parked outside, I knew he was alone."

"Bitch, I would have given you a heads up. Now, you better tell me why you're crying because if it was something Rylo did, I'm beating his ass," she said, and we both erupted in laughter.

I loved having Royce around because she never allowed me to be sad. At times, I felt like I depended on her to keep me together, and I prayed I wasn't a burden. I could be a lot to deal with, but Royce never treated me any differently. She wasn't like everyone else who constantly told me I was crazy.

"No, he didn't do anything. This pregnancy has my emotions all out of whack." That much was true. My emotions had been all over the place. I was really fucked up over Baron, but I had to pull myself together. "Then, seeing Sterling brought back all kinds of painful memories."

Royce leaned over and gave me a hug. She had this warm and gentle spirit that calmed me. I understood why people always wanted her around, Alex included.

"Bitch, you could've told me him and Arrington fuck around."

"I didn't think anything of it. Arrington thinks Rylo is her man. She be running all around town, telling people he pays all her bills. He probably does, but that's beside the point. She has people in the streets thinking they have been in a relationship all this time," Royce revealed.

"All this time?"

"Yes, like four years."

"Wait a minute. You're telling me they've been fucking around for four years, and he still ain't asked her to be his girl?"

"That's exactly what I'm saying, Chi. She's delusional."

Arrington wasn't a factor in my life, so I rarely spoke on her. Royce wasn't the type to tell people's business, so for her to spill the tea, Arrington must have pissed her off. I think she was finally starting to realize that me and Arrington would never be cool. That hoe wasn't worthy enough to be considered my stepsister. Years of verbal abuse from her and Tracy would forever be engraved in my memory, and there wasn't any coming back from that.

"Did you need to stop anywhere before I drop you off?"

"Yes. I need to get some fries from Wendy's. That's all I've been craving lately." I sighed.

I was ready for all this shit to be over. I wanted Baron and his brother to find another place to live. Shit, they could get a place together for all I cared. I just wanted him to get the hell away from me.

"You still haven't told Baron about the baby?"

I knew Royce was going to ask me about that. At that point, Baron could kiss my ass. I refused to have a baby by a cheating ass nigga. We never planned for this anyway. All I wanted to do was move on with my life and be happy. The thought of having to be responsible for another human overwhelmed me.

"No, not yet. I'm still thinking about it," I lied.

When we pulled up to my apartment, I pulled my luggage out of the backseat and gave Royce a hug. She just didn't know how much I appreciated her. Outside of my father, she was the only person I had in this world.

"Thanks again, Royce. I'll call you after I get up from my nap."

That was part of the truth. If Baron was there, I was going to fuck his ass up. This nigga thought he had something nice planned for me. Wait until he saw what the fuck I had planned for him. I should've paid for another day at the hotel, but I wasn't about to keep running from my own damn house. It was bad enough I came home from Houston early and didn't tell anybody.

Everything had finally started to make sense. Baron thought I was cheating because he had already been doing his dirt.

An unsettled feeling came over me as I approached my apartment. Nothing looked out of place, but I couldn't shake the feeling that something was terribly wrong. I started to call Baron, but I remembered I had been ignoring him. He didn't know I was pissed, but he was about to find out. Pulling out my keys, I unlocked the door and screamed. Baron was lying on the couch, holding his arm as blood oozed out.

"Oh, my God, Baron! What happened?"

Running over to him, I tried to find the wound to apply pressure. There was blood all over the couch, and I prayed it wasn't as bad as it looked. Baron might have been a piece of shit, but I didn't want anything bad to happen to him.

"Baby, run!"

I was caught off guard when someone grabbed me from behind. I tried to scream, but as soon as I did, someone placed their hand over my mouth. The look of horror on Baron's face scared the hell out of me. What type of shit had he been getting into that caused him to get shot? I tried my best to get away from my attacker, but my fear started to get the best of me. I wanted to believe I could fight this man, but I knew he was much stronger than me. I tried to use my body weight and fall to the ground, but he had me in what felt like a death grip. Panic washed over me as my stomach did somersaults. Was this God's way of punishing me? Because if it was, this shit wasn't funny.

*The night Sterling raped me started playing in my head. He had been the charming star athlete at Tilman, and every girl wanted him. When he chose me, I was surprised because all my life, I'd been the fat girl who nobody wanted. It didn't matter that I was pretty. Sterling made me feel like none of that mattered.*

*He invited me out to a frat party, and I gladly accepted. I remembered spending all the money I had left in my bank account to buy an outfit. I even paid to get my makeup done. At that time, my self-esteem was low, so I had to make sure I looked like all the other girls, even if that wasn't my style.*

"If you try to scream again, bitch, I'ma kill you," the voice behind me said, pulling me from my thoughts.

Somehow, I'd slipped into a dark place and hadn't realized it. It happened often, but me being attacked must have triggered it. My breathing became rapid as I struggled to stay calm.

"Man, let her go. I told you I don't know where Byron or your money is. We ain't got shit to do with this. Just let my girl go," Baron pleaded.

So, this had something to do with Byron? I told Baron that boy wasn't going to change. Byron ran the streets all day and night like he didn't have a working tow truck. He didn't promote or market his business but expected to be making money. The only thing I ever agreed with their mother, Janice, on was the fact that Byron wasn't ready to change.

"Well, you better tell Byron to give me my shit. I might just take some collateral." He laughed.

When he first grabbed me, I swore I heard a second person, but I wasn't sure. I couldn't see his face since he was holding me from behind. Something told me to look to my left. As I slowly turned my head, I locked eyes with none other than Sterling fucking White.

*TO BE CONTINUED...*

# Also By Tasha Mack

Made in the USA
Monee, IL
03 October 2023

43894660R00085